JC BRATTON'S

THiNGS THaT GO BUMP iN THe NiGHT

VOLUME ONE: URBAN LEGENDS

JC BRATTON'S THINGS THAT GO BUMP IN THE NIGHT

VOLUME ONE: URBAN LEGENDS

BLUE MILK Publishing

ISBN-13: 978-1-7367715-3-2 (hardback)

ISBN-13: 978-1-7367715-4-9 (paperback)

ISBN-13: 978-1-7367715-5-6 (digital online)

Library of Congress Control Number: 2023919709

First printing edition, October 2023

Second printing edition, February 2024

Third printing edition, March 2025

Blue Milk Publishing: San Jose, California

WHO'S AT THE DOOR?

JC Bratton

WHO'S AT THE DOOR?

"This eerie novella and its smart adolescent sleuths will
appeal to younger teen fans of spooky stories."
— *Publisher's Weekly*

★★★★
"A spine-tingling supernatural thriller…"
— *Self-Publishing Review*

Copyright © 2020 by JC Bratton

WHO'S AT THE DOOR?

Due to an unfortunate accident, 17-year old Jamie Patterson had to decline a Hawaiian cruise with her family and stay at home. To protect the home while they were away, Jamie's father installed a video-monitored doorbell. Little did Jamie know that the device that was supposed to guard her would ultimately become her biggest nightmare. At 3:33 PM, Jamie received a notification on her phone that the doorbell rang; however, there was no one at the door...With the aid of her estranged boyfriend, Jamie unravels a mystery more dangerous than she could possibly imagine in order to answer one simple question: "Who's at the door?"

PROLOGUE

MAY 20, 2017

My head was spinning as I heard the sirens around me. I could feel the blood drip from my forehead, and I couldn't move my left leg. There were lights around me as I laid on a gurney. Apparently, I had hit something or *someone*. I just remember being tired after a long night. We just graduated, and I was at Shelly's late-night party. I had a fight with Mark. It started raining when I hit the road, and it was very hard to see.

"Miss, I'm Sheriff King. I know things may be a bit fuzzy, but can you tell me what happened?" The Sheriff had a sympathetic look on his face as he hovered over me.

"I — I can't remember. Did I hurt someone?" I asked.

"No, Miss; just one big dent on your front bumper from you hitting that tree over yonder. Looks like you weren't drinking, which is good. Did you get distracted somehow?"

A tree? Distracted? Something distracted me, but I just don't remember what.

"I'm sorry, Sheriff, I am not sure," I struggled to talk, as I was in so much pain. "I do remember being tired. I guess I must have drifted off the road."

I remember a feeling; a feeling of being frightened. It wasn't the fear of hitting a tree. It was a ghastly fear, something that tears into your soul...

CHAPTER 1

"Bye, Jamie! We'll text you as soon as we land."

I waved good-bye as they climbed into the car. Mom always wanted to go to Hawaii, and Dad was finally able to break free from his robotics research company long enough to take Mom on her dream vacation for their 20th anniversary. They were such a cute couple: Dad was 6 feet, 4 inches tall and Mom was barely 5-feet. I met them in the middle at 5 feet, 7 inches with long brown hair and large brown eyes.

When I closed the door, the house felt a bit cold, but I was glad to have it to myself for the next 2 weeks. It's been about a month and a half since my accident, and now I am in a walking boot. I didn't feel that I was in any condition to enjoy Hawaii with Mom and Dad. They wanted to cancel the trip, but I vehemently said no. It was their anniversary, and I knew how much this trip meant to Mom. Besides, spending a few weeks at home wasn't so bad, especially for a homebody like me.

Mark was in town, and he offered to help me out. He lives across the street, and my parents adore him. Mark is over 6 feet tall with dark brown hair and sky blue eyes. We were high school sweethearts. However, he's moving to California to attend Caltech in September, and I am going to stay local and attend Ohio State. They say long-distance relationships never work. So, I ended our relationship the night of the accident. Mark wasn't happy about it. He's been pining for me ever since.

We live in the suburbs outside of Columbus. Our home is quite spacious: 3 bedrooms, 2.5 baths, 2,500 square feet. What I love about the house is the small loft on top of the stairwell. I sort of made that area my mini-lounge. My mom had a huge collection of suspense stories that she let me keep. For several hours, I curled up on my futon and became immersed in a young adult thriller about a babysitter being threatened by a mysterious stranger when it happened: it was 3:33 PM, and my phone chimed to tell me that it sensed motion at the door. Dad installed this fancy motion sensor gadget to catch package thieves. "You can never be too careful," Dad always said.

With the clunky walking boot, I was in no condition to go running down the stairs. The app on my phone would have to do. When I loaded the app, I saw the front porch with a view of both the street and Mark's house. Nothing seemed out of the ordinary except that *there was no one at the door.* How could that be? The camera must have picked up *something*. That feeling was back. That feeling I had 6 weeks ago — *that night*.

———

I wobbled down the stairs as fast as I could and opened the door. I was startled by Mark.

"Hey! Wow — I didn't mean to scare you!" Mark exclaimed.

I was relieved to see Mark, but I paused to look around the porch area; again, nothing looked out of the ordinary.

"Mark, did you see anyone drop by?" I asked.

Mark shook his head. I looked back at the app on my phone; it indicated that there was a new motion, being that Mark was at the porch.

"Oh, you have that app that lets you know if there is motion at your door, huh? It's pretty cool," Mark said.

"Well, yeah, but I am a little confused. At 3:33, the app told me that someone was at the door. I didn't see anyone in the video. Can you look?"

I showed the video to Mark.

"Maybe it was just the breeze? It's been a bit windy today; maybe that set off the motion sensor?"

Mark investigated the doorbell and the device sensor. Nothing seemed out of the ordinary. But, how could it be?

"Not sure what to tell you, Jamie, but everything seems normal."

Everything did seem normal, and I was definitely feeling better now that Mark was there.

"Oh well. A false positive. No sense in worrying about it, right?" I shrugged. "Hey, why did you drop by, Mark?"

"Oh, no reason. Just wanted to see how you were doing. Your parents left for their trip, so I thought you could use some company."

Mark came into the house, and we settled on ordering a pizza and watching some TV. The History Channel was playing a special on ghosts. Parapsychologists discussed various theories, one of which proposed that apparitions are inter-dimensional beings who are living in another time and space: the multiverse theory, as it was called. In it, ghosts may simply be beings temporarily visible to us as dimensions get crossed up, giving us a glimpse into another world.

"Maybe that's what happened, Jamie? Maybe a being from another dimension rang your doorbell?" Mark smirked with amusement. He could be a smart ass at times. I shook my head at him.

"Seriously. In another dimension, you and I are not sitting on this couch but could be in Paris having a romantic stroll by the River Seine." Mark moved closer to me on the couch. "I could be leaning over to you like this."

Mark's blue eyes pierced into mine as he gently placed his hand on my face, slowly running his thumb on my lower lip. I could feel my heart beating faster. I never knew that Mark could be this romantic. Mark's lips were ready to touch mine when the doorbell rang. My phone buzzed indicating motion at the door. It was the pizza delivery guy.

———

Mark and I went back to watching TV and began eating the pizza. I wasn't brave enough to bring up what almost happened, and neither was Mark. Maybe it's for the best. I kept reminding myself that long distance relationships don't work. It's like what happened with my friend Shelly last summer. She met a really great guy who was visiting his cousins. They had a whirlwind romance for two months. He "promised" to write, and she "promised" to visit him over one of the breaks. It just wasn't meant to be, I guess.

Mark switched over to the local news. They run a special on Saturdays called *Missing* to discuss ongoing missing persons investigations in the area. There was a report of a girl, age 13, named Mary Montgomery of Edenvale. Her parents were unknown; her guardian, Ross Montgomery, came on the screen: a bearded man in his mid-50s who looked a bit like Obi-Wan Kenobi in the original *Star Wars*. It was the middle of the night, and Ross heard a loud thump in the hallway. He went over to check on Mary, but she had vanished. A photo of her appeared on the screen, and a chill came down my spine. She had pale skin and long, dark hair that seemed to cover her face slightly. She was wearing a white blouse and had an empty smile. Ross Montgomery indicated that he remembered that his clock had read 3:33 AM when he heard the thump on May 20th. My heart started to pound really fast, and I dropped my drink on the floor.

"Whoa! Hey, let me help you clean that up!" Mark reached over for some napkins. "Are you okay, Jamie? Looks like you saw a ghost."

"I think I just did," I said softly.

CHAPTER 2

MAY 20, 2017

just can't do this Mark," I said with tears in my eyes.

"Jamie, I — I love you," Mark declared. "We have gone over this a hundred times. I am not going to give up on us. Yes, it's a chance of a lifetime to intern at the Jet Propulsion Lab. I have to see it through. But, I am coming back for you and will be here every summer. Please, please don't give up on us."

"I need time to think, Mark. I can't breathe right now." I ran over to my car as fast as I could. Mark tried to stop me, but it was too late as I sped off Shelly's driveway.

It began raining really hard. Mark had warned me that I needed to put some water repellent on the car. The windshield was so dirty. It was the first time it rained in a long time. Tears were still falling from my eyes.

"God, why is it so chilly?" I muttered to myself. I turned on the heater. It was the end of May for crying out loud. As I reached over for the heater, I accidentally tipped over the coffee sitting in my cup holder from earlier in the day.

"Dammit!" I yelled. I looked down briefly to see what damage I had done. Thankfully, the lid was still in place and nothing had spilt. When I looked up, however, there she was staring at me coldly from my rear-view mirror: a ghostly girl with dark hair covering her face.

I screamed in terror! Then, I swerved off the road and hit a large tree. My airbag went off. Before I blacked out, I glanced at the car clock as blood dripped down my face: 3:33 AM.

CHAPTER 3

I t had to be Mary. I just know it. But why? How is it even possible?

"Hey, Jamie — you ok?" Mark looked over at me with deep concern.

"You aren't going to believe this, Mark, I — wait, it's just too improbable…" I couldn't believe I was actually thinking about it. Did I see a ghost?

"No, no. I need to know what's going on in there," Mark said, pointing at my head. "What is it, Jamie?"

"The girl. Mary Montgomery. I have *seen* her. She was — she was in the car with me the night of the accident. She just suddenly appeared and was staring at me from my rear-view mirror. Her face startled me. I don't know how she got into my car. She's what distracted me and made me hit the tree. She put me in this walking boot." I looked down at my fractured leg and began to cry.

"Shh, shh." Mark moved next to me and put his arm around my shoulder. "Jamie, look, there must be a logical explanation. Maybe she ran away from home? Maybe she hid in your car, and you didn't notice her? You were really angry at the party. You may have already been too distracted to notice that she was in your back seat — a stowaway."

It was nice being in Mark's arms. I did miss him. He always knows how to make me feel better.

"Jamie, look, maybe we should go to Edenvale tomorrow and talk to Ross Montgomery? We should tell him that you saw Mary. I know that you don't remember much, but maybe it can help solve some of the mystery?"

"Can you stay over tonight, Mark?" Mark nodded and continued to hold me. I kept having an unsettling feeling. It's been so cold in the house, as if there was *something* there.

Mark and I fell asleep on the living room sofa. Some infomercial aired on the TV and the lights were still on. My phone started to buzz. The buzzing woke me up, and my movement caused Mark to wake up.

"Oh wow. What time is it?" Mark asked while yawning and still half asleep.

I looked at my phone. It was 3:33 AM, and there was a message saying there was motion at the door. I played the video, and I screamed in terror! There was someone at the door: it was Mary Montgomery, covered in blood.

"Mark! *She's* at the door!" I shouted.

"Stay here, Jamie!" Mark rushed to the door with one of our fire-irons in his hand. He looked into the peephole, and there was no one there. Mark then opened the door. Still no one; just a breeze.

"Hey! Hey! Anyone there?" Mark yelled out. We could hear the dogs barking a few doors down. The neighborhood looked peaceful. Mark closed the door and locked it.

I was frozen on the couch. I couldn't move.

"Jamie, let me see your phone." I was speechless. Mark then discovered my phone on the floor. He looked at the video history, and there was *nothing*. Nothing since the pizza delivery guy.

"Jamie, I don't see the video. You *did* see a video, right?" Mark showed me the phone and the history. There was no video. I was in shock.

"Mark — Mark, I swear to you, there was a video. It was Mary Montgomery at the door. She was covered in blood! I'm not crazy, Mark." I started crying.

"You *aren't* crazy, Jamie. I believe you. You saw something. But, the video is gone. Could it be that you were having a nightmare?"

"No, Mark, it was *real*. And, Mark, 3:33 AM. AGAIN. 3:33 AM. Why, Mark? Why is this happening to me?"

CHAPTER 4

We couldn't sleep, so we just took off in Mark's car and headed to Edenvale. My parents had texted me to let me know they made it to Hawaii and were settled in. Wifi would be spotty on the cruise ship, but they would check-in when they could.

"Jamie, we are having a lot of connectivity issues," Dad texted. "The doorbell app isn't loading video. We hope you are okay."

I wasn't about to tell him about Mary Montgomery. I wouldn't know where to begin.

Mark was driving and had turned the radio over to the local news in case there were any reports even remotely related to runaways, pranksters ... *something* to explain what I had experienced.

"Breaking news: a body was discovered, badly decomposed. It appears to be that of a young girl. The speculation is that it may be the body of 13-year old Mary Montgomery of Edenvale, who has been missing since May 20. The body was discovered about 15 miles north near Waverly Lake. Stay tuned to WKAM for the latest."

"Wait, that's near where you had your accident, Jamie!" Mark exclaimed. "We need to head up there, now!"

Mark made a u-turn and headed up the highway towards Waverly Lake.

———

It didn't take long to find where the authorities were investigating the location of the young girl's body. We pulled over to the side of the road and proceeded as far as we could until we were stopped by the county Sheriff. I recognized him; he was the one who questioned me when I had my accident: Sheriff King.

Sheriff King was a portly man in his 50s. He was well-respected in the community, but he was known to have some unorthodox investigation techniques. His deputies joked that he was "Fox Mulder's redneck cousin."

"This is official law enforcement business. Head back to your car, kids," Sheriff King said sternly and only halfway paying attention to who we were.

"We apologize, Sheriff, but we have some information on Mary Montgomery," Mark stated firmly. "My girl — um — friend here believes she saw Mary the night of her disappearance."

The Sheriff looked over at us.

"Wait, I recognize you. You were the girl who ran into the tree; I think about 10 minutes down the road here." The Sheriff pointed up ahead.

"Yes, Sheriff King. My name is Jamie. I was distracted and ran into the tree. But, I think I know why. I saw Mary in my rearview mirror. She must have been sitting in my back seat." Shivers came down my spine as I spoke those words.

"I know you were having problems remembering what happened to you that night, Miss Jamie," the Sheriff said. "It just doesn't seem possible based on everything we know about Mary." The Sheriff halted his conversation with us as the reporters were growing more anxious. "You'll have to excuse me, kids. If you want to make a statement, stop by my station later this afternoon, and we can talk then." The Sheriff walked toward the crowd that was gathering.

"There is something not right here, Jamie," Mark said. "We'll go by the station later, but let's see what we can find on our own in the meantime."

———

We headed over to see if we could meet up with Ross Montgomery as originally planned.

There was only one Ross Montgomery listed for Edenvale. He lived in a modest neighborhood on Primrose Drive. There were police cars parked in his driveway, so it obviously wasn't the best time for us to chat with him. Instead, we parked down the road and began walking along the sidewalk. About 5 houses down, we saw two teenage girls most likely coming back from shopping, as they were carrying large department store bags. One girl was of legal driving age, maybe around 16, and the other, possibly her sister, looked about Mary's age. They gave us a wondering look as we walked down the sidewalk. Being one not to shy away from a conversation, Mark decided to engage with the young ladies.

"Excuse me. Do you happen to know someone named Mary Montgomery?" The two girls giggled a bit, taken aback by how handsome Mark was. I was used to it. He was definitely easy on the eyes.

"Yeah. Beth here went to school with her," the older girl said carefree. Beth blushed a little and then nodded at Mark and I.

"Beth, what can you tell us about Mary?" Mark asked without hesitation.

"Well, Mary didn't have many friends. She was skinny and awkward; the quiet type. Guess that's a deadly combination to become the butt of jokes." Beth looked a bit sad as she continued. "I talked to her now and then. I don't care what people think of me. I believe in the Golden Rule."

Beth continued. "The worst thing happened a week before school let out. Mary got her period. She was spotting like crazy and didn't know it. Someone played a prank on her. Kinda *Carrie*-esque. They stuffed her locker with tampons and wrote 'Bloody Mary' across her locker door."

I gasped. "My God, that's awful!"

"Yeah, the teachers were not happy," Beth said. "They couldn't prove who did it, though. They let Mary stay home for the remainder of the school year. And that's about all I know."

"Beth, Erica!" a voice from inside the adjacent house called out.

"Be right there, Mom," Erica said. "We have to get going. Our mom is calling." Erica raced into the house. Beth headed to the door but then looked over at me for a second with a puzzled expression. She then shook it off and headed inside. As Beth walked in, I noticed a sign that said "Reese" above the front door. As I looked a little more carefully, I noticed that the house was equipped with the same doorbell monitor that I had; a chill went down my spine.

"Bloody Mary," Mark said, interrupting my thoughts. "Hey, don't you remember that game that you and I would play when we were younger? You had that old, creepy mirror in your attic, and we would go up there and speak the name 'Bloody Mary' into it three times in a row to see if we can summon a spirit. Remember that?"

"Yeah, I remember," I said. "Even though you said it never worked, I remember thinking I saw something appear the third time we tried. God, that really freaks me out, Mark, to think about it!"

I think I was around Mary's age when it happened. It was Halloween. I was dressed as a zombie bee, and Mark was a beekeeper. Yes, we did silly things like that. It had been about 5 or more years since we played Bloody Mary. It never worked, but when Mark wanted to try this time, something felt a bit off. We were supposed to be asleep. It was really late at night. In fact, it could have been around 3 in the morning.

"No, Mark, I don't feel like playing," I said objectionably.

"Come on! It's Halloween. We are all entitled to one good scare," Mark said convincingly. "Also, your parents plan to have a garage sale and most of the stuff in the attic are going away. Let's give the mirror one last try!"

As thirteen-year-olds, we were beginning to develop feelings for each other. Innocent crushes, but we knew something was there. Mark's charm made it easy for him to persuade me to play along.

"All right, but I really am getting tired."

Carrying a lighter and some candles, we climbed up to the attic where my parents stored the old mirror. It was very tall, about 7 feet. It looked like something out of *Harry Potter*. It was a family heirloom, passed on by my great-great-grandmother. Rumor has it that she was a heretic. My dad, being the scientist he was, didn't believe in "hocus pocus." So the mirror was placed in the attic to be sold off one day with all the other "pieces of junk."

Mark lit the candles. I saw our reflection in the mirror; two kids in their costumes. As I looked closer at my reflection, I thought I saw something behind me; a shadow of sorts. I gasped and quickly looked behind me. Of course, nothing was there, and I gathered my breath.

"Hey, you ok?" Mark asked with concern.

"Yeah." I shook it off but still felt a bit unsettled.

"Okay. Then let's begin," Mark said in a serious tone. "Let's say it together ... 1, 2, 3..."

"Bloody Mary," we said calmly together.

"Bloody Mary," we chanted again. The attic temperature felt like it dropped a few degrees.

After a slight pause, Mark and I looked at each other then turned to the mirror.

"Bloody Mary."

To Mark's disappointment, all that appeared in the mirror were our reflections.

"Dammit," Mark said disappointingly. "Come on, Jamie. Guess it's a night of tricks rather than treats." Mark began walking back to the ladder.

"Hey wait, we need to blow out the candles." As I looked back to blow them out, there she was. Her face was as white as snow, and she had blood-red lips. I screamed at the top of my lungs and passed out on the floor.

The next morning, I woke up in bed. According to Mark, he thinks the scream came from me tripping over the rug on the attic floor and burning my hand on one of the candles. I was known to be a bit clumsy. My parents scolded us for being up in the attic so late by ourselves. They had their garage sale, and the mirror was picked up by someone from out of town. No one believed that I saw anything; after a while, I became convinced that I didn't see anything either. Until now...

———

"Well, I believed I saw *something* in the mirror that night, Mark," I said sadly.

"Something did happen, Jamie," Mark said. "And maybe all of this is tied together. You know I am the practical type, a lot like your dad. There has to be a logical explanation to it all. Let's grab a bite to eat and head over to the Sheriff's station. We can tell him everything we know, and let's see if any of this adds up."

I thought that was a good idea, and we took off to downtown. Beth looked out of her bedroom window at our passing car. She then turned around and took out her hairbrush. She walked over and looked at her reflection in the antique 7-foot tall mirror that her family acquired in a garage sale 5 years before and smiled.

CHAPTER 5

Mark and I headed over to our favorite burger joint and grabbed some sliders. It was good comfort food considering what we had gone through in the last 24 hours.

"Hey, did you notice that Beth and Erica have the same doorbell monitor that I have?" I asked Mark.

"Yeah, now that I think about it, I saw that, too," Mark said with his mouth full. "Beth said she knew Mary from school. You know, let me see if she has a Facebook page. Beth Reese of Edenvale…"

Mark took out his phone and browsed through various Facebook profiles and found Beth. It was a selfie of she and Erica. Beth had some public wall posts. In fact, one was from yesterday, around 3:40 PM: it read, "This motion monitor sucks. It tells me someone is at the door, but look..." She shared the video from her phone. There was no one at the door. The timestamp was 3:33 PM.

"Oh my God! What time is it now?" I asked Mark frantically.

"It's almost 3:30 PM now. I wonder…" Mark's sentence was interrupted by a buzz from my phone. A motion detection … at 3:33 PM.

"Oh no, Mark!" I didn't dare to look at my phone.

"Give me your phone," Mark demanded. I handed it over to him. A pale look came over his face. "What the hell?"

I had to look. I moved next to Mark and saw the video. A piece of paper was blowing in the wind. The paper blew in front of the camera and read "BETH" in blood red.

"We need to go back and see Beth. *Now*."

———

Beth was in her room, fully satisfied after the big meal that her mom cooked. The girls' mom had to leave the house to pick up their father, as his car was in the shop. Beth put on her headphones. She was drifting to sleep but was awakened by a series of tapping noises, as if someone was tapping on glass. Beth removed her headphones and looked around. She didn't see anything out of the ordinary. Her window was open to let in a breeze and everything looked to be in place. Shrugging it off, Beth put her headphones back on. The tapping grew louder, and then there was a voice, a woman's voice: "Beth…"

Beth shot out of her bed and screamed, "Who's there?!" Her heart was racing and her breathing grew harder. Nothing. There was no one in the room. Terrified, Beth raced to her bedroom door only to find that she couldn't open it. It was jammed. The tapping continued, and the voice grew louder: "Beth…"

Now Beth realized where the sound was coming from. Beth was facing the door and very slowly turned her head to view the mirror in the room…

———

We raced to Beth's house. Fortunately, we didn't get a speeding ticket. Mark jumped out of the car. With my walking boot on, I hobbled as fast as I could to the front door. Mark rang the door-bell and knocked really hard.

"Coming…" Erica's voice didn't sound anxious or concerned.

"Erica, hurry up! It's Mark and Jamie. From earlier…" Mark stated in panic.

Erica opened the door, and Mark raced inside.

"Beth! Beth!" Mark shouted.

"Whoa — wait, what's going on?" Erica's eyes were wide open with concern.

"We are afraid something could be wrong with Beth. Where is she?" Mark asked.

"She should be upstairs in her room," Erica said with a very confused look on her face.

Mark ran up the stairs. Erica and I followed as fast as we could.

"Oh my God!" Mark shouted. Beth's door was open, and she was unconscious on the floor. Her left arm was exposed, and there appeared to be marks burned into her skin, as if *someone* grabbed her arm and squeezed it with something that was red hot.

"Beth! Beth!" Erica cried out as she ran over to her sister. Slowly Beth regained consciousness. Erica and Mark picked Beth up and moved her onto her bed. Erica told me to grab some cream and a washcloth from the bathroom down the hall. I returned with the items and a cup of tap water. Erica thanked me and had Beth take a small sip of water. As Beth sipped her water, she whispered, "Mirror."

"Mirror?" Mark questioned.

"The mirror," Beth said more deliberately.

I glanced around and noticed that there was a large object behind the door; it looked familiar. I looked behind the door to see the same 7-foot mirror that had been in my parents' attic!

"Mark! It's my parents' old mirror!" I shouted.

Mark came over and stared at it.

"When did you get this mirror?" Mark asked Erica.

"My parents bought it in an antique sale about 5 years ago, I think," Erica explained. "For some reason, Beth was mesmerized by it, so Mom and Dad let her have it."

"The mirror..." Beth said again.

"Yes, Beth, what happened?" Erica asked gently.

"I — I don't remember. Ouch." Beth felt the burn marks. "I just remember that I saw something in the mirror and then blacked out."

The mirror didn't look out of the ordinary. It was maybe just a bit more worn than might be expected.

"How did you know to come back here and that Beth was in trouble?" Erica asked with concern on her face.

Mark looked over at me, as if hesitant to explain the situation, but he continued.

"Jamie has a motion detector, just like the one you have installed in your house, at her place. It was set off today, and a piece of paper came flying onto the screen that said 'BETH.' Do you have the video, Jamie?"

I took out my phone, and loaded the app, but the video was gone! I gasped.

"Mark! The video is gone!"

Mark grabbed my phone, and the last video was the pizza guy at the door from last night.

"Erica, Beth. We swear to you. There was a video..." Mark was stopped mid-sentence by Erica.

"I think you both should leave," Erica said with a suspicious look. "Our parents are going to be home soon." She looked over at her sister, who still seemed in shock.

"Something is not right here. We want to help," I pleaded.

"No, please go. We appreciate your concern, but please," Erica said boldly.

We honored her wishes and walked out of the house.

"This is crazy, Mark. I feel like this is one big nightmare."

"Let's go see Sheriff King," Mark said sternly. "We need to get to the bottom of this."

———

As we pulled into the station, Sheriff King arrived simultaneously. We stopped him as he got out of his vehicle.

"Sheriff! We need to speak with you now!" Mark urged. "We have some very important information about the Mary Montgomery case."

"Okay, son, calm down," Sheriff King said while patting Mark on the shoulder. "You and Miss Jamie here can come inside my office, and we can chat."

We sat down in Sheriff King's office. It was a medium-sized office. He had a library of books about sociopaths, unsolved murders, small-town crimes … and one that stood out in particular was titled *Hanako-San: Myth or Reality?*

Mark and I went into detail about the events of the last day and a half. The Sheriff didn't look at all suspicious about what we were telling him. In fact, he seemed intrigued.

"Beth Reese," Sheriff King muttered. "Well, we questioned her when Mary disappeared. She told you that she befriended Mary? Well, that's not what we gathered. We have some reason to believe that she may have been the mastermind behind the 'Bloody Mary' incident."

Mark and I looked at each other in amazement.

"Beth is very popular at the school. She's been known to be kind of mean. My son goes to school with Erica, and he has seen how the two girls behave. They tend to make fun of others who are a little awkward, like Mary was.

"Mr. Reese, the girls' father, is the Principal at the school, and there is a chance he knew that Beth was guilty of the bullying. This is all speculation. We don't have any proof. I mean, I shouldn't even tell you what I am telling you right now.

"Now, this incident regarding the mirror and the burn marks… Well, I owe the Reeses a visit. I'll see what I can gather."

"What do you think this all means, Sheriff?" I asked. "I mean, everything that happened with my accident, the videos, the mirror... Is there a logical explanation?"

The Sheriff turned his head over to his library of books. "Miss Jamie, as you can see, I read a lot of books on unsolved mysteries and even on the occult. I do believe you experienced *something*. Hopefully, there is a logical explanation."

The Sheriff took down our contact information and said he would give us a call. He seemed to sympathize with us. We definitely wouldn't expect him to share as much as he did, as this was an on-going investigation. However, he was as keen as we were to get this mystery solved.

CHAPTER 6
MAY 14, 2017

"Mary, it's time to get ready for school!" Ross Montgomery blurted from the kitchen.

Mary Montgomery, at age 13, had gone through more than anyone her age could imagine. She never knew her mother and father; she only knew the Montgomerys. Ross worked from home as a graphic designer. He was a loving man and did the best he could to raise Mary as his own. He and his wife were unable to have children, so they adopted Mary when she was 4. When Mary turned 7, Ross's wife, Grace, died of ovarian cancer at 45 years old. She left the family with a small amount of savings from an inheritance she had received. This was money that Ross set aside for Mary to use to go to college.

Mary never asked for much. She missed Grace, but Ross was a responsible and attentive guardian. He wasn't exactly the most fashionable man, and he didn't keep up on the latest pop culture trends. So, Mary naturally tended to follow his lead. At school, the girls would pick on her because she appeared uncomfortable in her own skin. Mary was thin and wasn't developing at the rate of many others, like Beth Reese, for example. Mary's big green eyes seemed much larger than her face.

Mary put on some jeans and a white shirt with a floral

pattern. She went downstairs, and Ross handed her a bag with her lunch. He kissed her on the cheek, and she walked over to the bus stop.

The sky was gray that morning. There was only about a week remaining for the school year. Along the route to the bus stop was the cemetery where Grace was buried. Out of the corner of her eye, Mary thought she saw someone: a mysterious woman wearing white. Maybe it was someone visiting a grave? The woman looked over at Mary. It was hard to see the woman's expression, but it gave Mary chills. Luckily, the bus arrived, and Mary hopped on as quickly as possible.

There was chatter as usual on the bus, and Mary sat alone as always — on the last seat in the back right side of the bus. Today felt a tad off. Mary began feeling dizzy and her stomach was cramping. Could it have been from breakfast? It was hard to tell. It was an unfamiliar feeling.

The bus stopped at the school, and Mary headed out. Beth Reese and her friends were talking about boys and playing on their smartphones. As Mary walked by, Beth and her friends looked up at her, turned to each other and started whispering and laughing. Mary just ignored them and headed to class. What Mary didn't realize was that she started spotting on her pants. Beth and her friends' laughing grew louder. Everyone outside stared at Mary and others joined in on the laughter when they noticed the bleeding. Still oblivious, Mary walked into the building. Mrs. Johnson was at her desk when she saw Mary walk in. She noticed the problem right away.

"Mary, dear, oh my! Looks like you have your period." Mrs. Johnson reached over into her desk and pulled out a maxi pad. "Here, dear, head to the ladies' room."

Mary felt so embarrassed. It all made sense to her now. She rushed into the bathroom, and Mrs. Johnson followed to make sure Mary was okay.

"I can call your father, and you can go home for the day."

Mary came out from the stall and nodded her head in agreement with Mrs. Johnson.

"I'll be right outside," Mrs. Johnson said.

Mary turned on the faucet, looking down in shame, tears continuing to pour down her face. When Mary looked up into the mirror, eyes foggy from the tears, she could have sworn she saw another girl staring back at her. She wasn't anyone Mary had recognized; she was very pale, had dark hair and black eyes. She was holding a brown, worn teddy bear. She put her index finger to her lips.

"Shhhhh!" the girl said.

Mary quickly turned around, and there was no one there; no one in any stalls either.

"You're imagining things, Mary," she thought.

Mrs. Johnson greeted Mary. She didn't think to bring up the girl in the mirror; there was already too much chaos.

"Can I go to my locker first? I need to take home some books," Mary said quietly.

Students scrambled to their first class of the day as Mrs. Johnson walked with Mary to her locker. Mrs. Johnson gasped in horror. There it was … in blood red: "BLOODY MARY" written boldly across Mary's locker. The door was ajar and tampons were flowing out from it. Students laughed as they slowly passed by for a better look, and the Principal, Mr. Reese, rushed over to break up the crowd.

"Settle down! Who is responsible for this?" Mr. Reese asked sternly. The laughter turned to silence. "Head to your classes now! Mary, walk with me."

Mr. Reese brought Mary and Mrs. Johnson to his office. Mary was speechless. She was hurt and angry. She had never felt this much rage before. She saw Beth Reese out of the corner of her eye. Beth's laughter came to a halt as she felt a chill down her spine when she saw the anger in Mary's eyes.

———

"Mr. Montgomery, we are going to get to the bottom of this fiasco," Mr. Reese assured Ross Montgomery, as he held Mary in his arms.

"You'd better get control of your students," Ross scolded. "I'll take this to the school board if I have to."

Ross and Mary walked out of Mr. Reese's office and headed out to their car.

As Ross started driving, he noticed how quiet Mary was.

"Mary, I can't believe how mean kids can be," Ross explained. "I can say that things will get better. I mean, back when I was in high school, I was picked on by the star basketball captain. Today, he's between jobs and has to find a way to provide child support for 3 children!"

Mary appreciated that Ross attempted to make her feel better, but she didn't feel like talking. She had a strong suspicion Beth was the mastermind behind the prank. Maybe Beth will get what's coming to her, she thought to herself.

CHAPTER 7

MAY 19, 2017

t had been a few days since the "Bloody Mary" incident. Mary wouldn't leave her room; she would spend the day in bed, periodically crying. Several family portraits sat on Mary's nightstand. Her favorite was a photo of Grace when she visited London. Grace had long, dark hair and a warm, beautiful smile.

"Why do the good ones get taken from us so soon?" Mary thought aloud.

The Montgomerys were not religious people; Ross considered himself agnostic, and Grace considered herself a "spiritual" person. Since Grace's passing, and as Mary grew older, the idea crossed her mind that maybe once you are gone you are really, truly gone: just a dark emptiness. If that was the case, then everything was insignificant, Mary conceded. Who cares about anything, really?

Mary climbed out of bed and walked to her window. It was a hazy, sunny day with a slight breeze. The leaves were rustling in the wind. For just a moment, Mary thought she could hear Grace's voice as the wind blew. It sounded like she was gently calling out "Mary." Mary shivered, but she shrugged it off.

"Just my imagination," Mary whispered.

Mary felt the need to go to the cemetery to visit Grace. She put on the summer hat that Grace used to wear and proceeded down the stairs to see Ross taking a nap. Normally, she went with Ross to visit Grace. Ross worked so hard, and he looked so peaceful. It was nice to see him take a quick break, which was the beauty of being able to work from home. Mary quietly snuck out through the back door.

"I won't be gone very long," Mary thought out loud. Ross would definitely be worried if she was, but Mary really wanted to just go on her own. She seemed drawn to do so, like something or *someone* called to her.

––––––

The cemetery was one of the oldest in the state. It was built during the Civil War. You can find headstones of Union lieutenants. For example, Adam Coleman, 2nd Lieutenant with Co D, 4th West Virginia Infantry Regiment; enlisted June 24, 1861. Mary knew some Civil War history from her social studies and civics classes: a nation divided. It's not much different from school, Mary thought: the Beth Reeses of the world oppressing, dividing...

Mary was deep in thought when she saw her again: the woman from a few days ago, wandering about the cemetery, about 100 yards away. She was a woman most likely in her late-30s with very long dark hair and a pale complexion. She was wearing a white gown, something you might wear to bed. She stopped and stared at Mary.

"Hello?" Mary asked. "Can I help you?"

The woman began to place her hand on her stomach and bent over. She seemed to be in pain.

Mary ran over to her to see if she could help.

CHAPTER 8

Mark and I decided that maybe we could try Ross Montgomery again, so we headed back to Primrose Drive. With all the excitement, I never noticed the old cemetery down the road. Out of the corner of my eye, I could have sworn I saw a dark-haired woman in white wandering past the graves.

"Hey, Mark. Let's stop here," I urged.

"Why do you want to visit this place?" Mark asked.

"I think I saw something," I claimed.

We parked along the street and headed into the cemetery. We saw old gravestones dating back to the Civil War. There were newer sections as well. People were still laid to rest here. As we were walking, I saw her: the woman in white.

"Mark! Look! There she is." I pointed over to the woman.

"Hello?" Mark asked the woman.

The woman did not reply back. In fact, she just ignored us and continued to walk away. We headed over to where we found her, but we stopped abruptly to find a summer hat on the ground jarred next to some bushes and a headstone: Grace Montgomery, Loving Wife and Mother.

I gasped, "Mary…"

Before I could say anything else, Mark's phone began to ring. It was Sheriff King.

"Kids, you'd better head back down to the station," Sheriff King said. "I have an important update that I think you all need to hear. It's best done in person."

———

We headed back to the Sheriff's station to be greeted immediately by Sheriff King. He took us back to his office and shut the door behind him.

"Well, I have some big news: Mary may still be alive!" Sheriff King exclaimed. "Seems the body was not of Mary but another girl who had been missing, a runaway."

Mark and I looked at each other in shock and wonder.

"And that's not everything," Sheriff King added. "I visited the Reese's home. The girls told me about the incident. Jamie, the mirror in Beth's room, that was in your family? What do you know about it?"

I was taken aback by the line of questioning, but I answered the best I could.

"Well, it came from my dad's family," I explained. "They have lived in the area for generations. There was a rumor that my great-great-grandmother was a heretic."

"Well, I can confirm that your great-great-grandmother, Margaret, was not a heretic," Sheriff King said in a serious tone. "Were you aware that she was not your great-great-grandfather's first wife?"

I looked up at Sheriff King, puzzled.

"That's news to me," I said curiously.

Sheriff King continued. "Well, there's a very bizarre story regarding the mirror and your ancestors. It's a bit tough to hear, but with everything that's going on, I think you need to learn the whole story. I uncovered these details from an old investigation that happened in this very county back in the early 1900s.

"Your great-great-grandfather, Elias Patterson, age 25, came to Edenvale, Ohio with no money but big ambitions as an inventor. He had befriended an older woman named Rosa Hunter, age 45, and they wed very quickly, after only 1 month of meeting. Rosa was widowed and gained a bit of wealth through her late husband. She had a daughter. Her name was Mary, age 13."

Mark and I looked at each other in wonder as Sheriff King continued.

"Rosa was very jealous of young Mary. She could see that Mary was growing into a very beautiful young woman. Not only did she have outer beauty, but she also had a strong will and was very caring. When Elias seemed to gravitate towards Mary, Rosa felt threatened and locked Mary in the attic for hours. There was a large mirror in the attic, and Mary would find herself trapped. She would beg her mother to let her out, but Rosa would keep Mary in the attic for hours, up until when Elias would arrive home. Rosa threatened Mary to never tell Elias what happened or there would be 'severe consequences.'"

"Oh my God," Mark interrupted. "This is terrible. Did Rosa ever get reported to the authorities?"

"She got what was coming to her," Sheriff King added with a smirk.

"One fateful day, Mary encountered Hanako-San. I don't know if you kids have noticed, but I have a book about this urban legend in my collection. Hanako-San is the Japanese legend of a little girl who haunts bathrooms. Seems Mary claimed, however, that Hanako-San appeared in the attic mirror. There is thought that the legend went beyond just haunting bathrooms: the spirit would torment young women in pain via any type of mirror.

"Elias would be working on his inventions very late at night in the outdoor shed that he turned into a workshop. Mary and Rosa got into a final argument, why so late at night, no one knows. It was so bad that it was heard by several neighbors. Rosa chased Mary up into the attic. Elias heard the commotion and ran up the stairs to stop it. Two concerned neighbors also joined Elias. When they got up to the attic, Rosa was there all alone: Mary had vanished. The time was 3:33 AM!

"Rosa pleaded to investigators that something came out of the mirror in the attic and grabbed Mary. No one believed her. There was enough town speculation that Rosa had been abusing Mary. Rosa and Elias divorced shortly after the disappearance of Mary. Mary Hunter's disappearance is one of our most infamous cold cases.

"From our records, Rosa was shamed and left town. She ended up passing away from a mysterious illness a few years later while living in Vermont. Elias moved to Columbus and met your blood great-great-grandmother. Jamie, you probably never learned about the Mary Hunter case, as Elias and Rosa's marriage records were destroyed in the Edenvale City Hall Fire of 1906."

Mark and I were left speechless. I had chills running down my spine. I started rubbing my arms, as I was feeling very cold.

"I told you all this was a lot to absorb," Sheriff King said, concerned. "Kids, I know you claimed that there were videos of Mary Montgomery. The camera you have at home, Jamie... I had one of my deputies stop by your house, and he looked at the model installed: it contains a mirror to help provide a wider view of the porch. I know this sounds crazy, and they call me the 'redneck Fox Mulder' around here, so I'll just say it: I think Mary Montgomery was taken by Hanako-San, or as you kids call her, 'Bloody Mary!'"

CHAPTER 9

MAY 19, 2017 @ 7 PM

"Mary, dinner time!" Ross had supper ready. Ross overslept and didn't hear Mary come back from her cemetery walk. When he woke up, Mary was sound asleep in bed.

When Mary didn't answer him, Ross put down the plates and headed up the stairs. Mary's door was closed.

"Knock, knock. Can I come in?" Ross asked.

"Come in," Mary said gently.

When Ross opened the door, Mary was dressed very peculiarly: all in white. The dress looked vintage, like something out of the early 1900s.

"Okay… new dress? When did you get that?" Ross asked.

"Oh, it's been in my closet," Mary said nonchalantly as she combed her long, dark hair and stared into the mirror by her dresser.

"Well, kids and their fashions, I guess. And, I know you have been through a lot," Ross shrugged.

"I have dinner ready. Come down when you are done with 'dress up,'" Ross said sarcastically.

When Ross left, Mary began smiling; not a pretty, healthy smile, but one of mischief. The person on the other side of the mirror was not Mary Montgomery. It was Mary Hunter, covered in blood, with Hanako-San behind her.

———

The graduation party was running really late; over 50 guests. It began at 7 PM, and now it was almost 2 AM on May 20. I can't believe how much energy everyone had. I'll probably be the most boring Freshman at Ohio State; falling asleep while everyone else is just starting their evenings.

I've known Shelly for as long as I can remember. She is a thin Indian girl with long black hair and about my height. Shelly's parties were always infamous for bringing out the wild side in people. She's been hosting gatherings since, well, her 5th birthday party.

Mark held me close to him all night. We looked like the perfect couple as always: "peas in a pod," they say. Why does he have to leave? I need him. I really do. I'll feel empty without him.

I needed some time to think. I excused myself and went to the bathroom. While I was away, Mark, Shelly, Shelly's younger sister Misha and Mark's friend Steve started joking aloud.

"Hey, Jamie and I used to play this game called 'Bloody Mary.' It was a total trip!" Mark was a bit tipsy. Yes, we weren't supposed to be drinking, but someone "happened" to add an extra element to one of the bowls of punch.

"I totally know that game!" Shelly interjected. "You know, guys, we can try it now. I have a long mirror in my room; come on!"

———

It was almost 3:30 AM. Ross had been tossing and turning all night.

"God, that dinner with Mary was so off," he thought. She

seemed like a totally different person; not the sweet girl he raised but someone who had confidence in a disturbing sort of way.

It was just too unsettling for Ross. He decided to get up and take a peek to see if Mary was sleeping peacefully.

THUD!

Ross rushed into Mary's room.

"MARY!!!! MARY!!!! Oh, God!"

The clock read 3:33 AM.

CHAPTER 10

"There's got to be a way to stop all of this, Sheriff." My voice was shaking as I said those words.

"Kids, I think there is a way," Sheriff King said. "One of these mirrors is the conduit. I suspect it's the one in Beth Reese's house. However, this is very dangerous. We want to get Mary Montgomery out of there alive."

"Alive?" Mark asked. "How do we even know Mary is truly alive? There is something evil here, Sheriff. And, I'm a practical man of science. I still feel that we are dealing with forces beyond our control."

"According to the Hanako-San legend, the victim is put into a trance," Sheriff King interjected. "There hasn't been a new 'victim' yet, as Beth Reese was able to escape. So, if we can get Mary out of there, she can be set free. Her physical body is *in* the mirror. Think of it as a portal to another dimension."

"So the secret is the *timing*," I added. "Think about it. 3:33. All the events happen at this specific time in the early morning or afternoon. Could we find a way to pull Mary out of the mirror?"

"There's only one way to find out." Sheriff King called to one of his deputies. "We are going to head over to the Reese house around 3 AM. The Reeses will be set up at a hotel. We'll wait for 3:33 AM, and get Mary out of there and keep the evil 'Marys' in the other dimension. Kids, we will set you up at the hotel, too."

―――――

We entered the car with Deputy Scott, a handsome man, maybe in his early-30s, muscular build, with dark hair and eyes. He was assigned to drive us to the hotel, which was about 5 blocks from the Reese home.

"All this 'Bloody Mary' mess is our fault," I explained to Mark. "Why did we play that silly game? I can't just let these good officers risk their lives for something we may have caused."

"Jamie, if you go, I go, too."

"Kids, you heard what Sheriff King said. This is for law enforcement to handle," Deputy Scott said sternly.

I shrugged at Mark, but he and I were both thinking the same thing: we'll find a way to the Reese house.

―――――

It was 3 AM. Deputy Scott was still in his car and was messaging someone on his phone. From the smile on his face, it was probably a girlfriend. He didn't see us sneak by him. Mark and I headed on foot over to the Reese residence. Of course, I was still wobbling in my walking boot, but we hoped to get there before 3:33 AM.

We passed by the old cemetery again.

"Mark, remember that lady we saw at the cemetery?" I asked. Mark nodded.

"Do you think she's tied into this somehow? I mean, we don't know much about Mary Hunter and Hanako-San."

"Possibly," Mark added. "Definitely a mysterious person, but

I don't know where to find her. Hard to tell anything in the cemetery when it's dark."

As we walked past, we didn't notice, but she was there, next to Grace's marker.

————

Sheriff King and his team set up shop in Beth's room. They lit candles around the mirror. Based on the Hanako-San legend, the conduit can be closed by breaking the mirror. They had a sledgehammer ready to hit as soon as they would be able to get Mary out of the mirror. Ross Montgomery waited behind the officers, hoping and praying Mary was still alive and well.

We were able to sneak in through the front door and climbed up the stairs to see the Sheriff and his team bracing for 3:33 AM. The mirror in the room began to liquify. Mary Montgomery's hand slowly began to appear when my phone started buzzing. Someone or *something* was at *my door*!

"Oh my God, Mark!" I exclaimed.

"Kids! What are you doing here?!" Sheriff King yelled while trying to grab onto Mary's hand.

Mark and I quickly watched the video. It was a note floating in blood-red letters: "JAMIE."

I dropped my phone and passed out on the floor.

EPILOGUE

The Bloody Mary incident was over. When I passed out, Sheriff King was able to grab Mary Montgomery out of the mirror. His team was able to destroy the mirror before anything or *anyone* else could come out.

Days had passed; no mysterious video alerts: just the pizza guy, Mark … and then my parents when they got back from Hawaii. Strangely, none of the mysterious videos loaded on my parents' phones. Needless to say, Mark and I kept the Bloody Mary incident to ourselves.

Sheriff King commended Mark and I on our bravery. Mary Montgomery was safe and had no recollection of the events. The last thing she remembered was visiting Grace at the cemetery. Beth learned her lesson: she was not "above" anyone else. The Sheriff's department decided to keep under wraps the "Bloody Mary" portion of the case. Instead, they said that Mary simply ran away and came back.

We were safe.

———

Shelly and I became roommates at Ohio State. Most of Shelly's furniture arrived today. Mark went to Caltech as planned, but, of course, we got back together. I mean, who can resist those sky blue eyes?

"Sweetie, I'm heading to the library," I told Mark on our video call.

"I miss you! Remember, I'll be over there in a few weeks." Mark blew me a virtual kiss. I grabbed it in the air and placed it near my heart.

There was some thunder crackling outside. Looks like a storm was coming. The clock read 12:33 PM on Mark's end. I keep forgetting he's 3 hours behind me. We ended our video call.

"Time to get ready for the library," I thought. I needed to fix my hair and put on a rain jacket. I closed the door behind me, as we had just added the large door mirror that Shelly brought over from her house. When I looked in the mirror, it was clear I wasn't alone. *She* was there: Bloody Mary, standing right behind me...

parasomnia

JC BRATTON

AUTHOR OF THE BEST-SELLING SHORT STORY
WHO'S AT THE DOOR?

PARASOMNIA

★★★★
"A mysterious and romantic ride."
— *Self-Publishing Review*

———

PARASOMNIA

Recent divorcée Alex Anderson suffers from hypnopompic hallucinations, parasomnias that take place between REM sleep and wakefulness. The hallucinations consist of rapid moving still images that appear before her eyes while closed. She encounters a still image of the most perfect man she has ever seen in her life. She later learns that this man was a real person, Dr. Scott Collier, who tragically died in a car accident. With the help of her friends, a psychologist, and clues left behind by a mysterious young woman, Alex learns that Scott may not be her "dream man" after all; instead, he could be her biggest nightmare.

par · a · som · ni · a

[/ˌperəˈsämnēə/] noun (medicine): a disorder characterized by abnormal or unusual behaviors of the nervous system during sleep.

————

"The man of my dreams has almost faded now. The one I have created in my mind. The sort of man each woman dreams of, in the deepest and most secret reaches of her heart." — Elise McKenna, *Somewhere in Time*

————

"Diabolical forces are formidable. These forces are eternal, and they exist today. The fairy tale is true. The devil exists. God exists. And for us, as people, our very destiny hinges upon which one we elect to follow." — Ed Warren, paranormal investigator

PROLOGUE
PARADOX

I had a difficult time sleeping ever since my dad passed. It was over four weeks ago; losing him was the worst loss I ever experienced — more difficult than the dissolution of my marriage. Although my eyes were billowy from all my tears, last night I was able to sleep a full five hours; a huge accomplishment. Upon waking, something very bizarre happened — before my closed eyes were a series of rapidly moving images in succession: crisp, high-resolution stills of unrelated people and places moving quickly along my field of vision. I had absolutely no idea what this was all about. It was a frightful but exciting feeling; paradoxical? Each image was engaging. The faces, the places — all were so very interesting. Then it happened: I saw *him*; he was the most perfect man I had ever seen in my life. He looked to be close to my age, maybe early 30s? He had fair skin, light brown hair, hazel eyes; there was a slight crease along his right cheek when he smiled. There was an innocence about him. I was instantly attracted to him, not just physically but in a magical sort of way. After about thirty-seconds, his image slowly faded away, and I woke up. Wow, I could not shake his image. *Who was he?*

PART ONE
LOSS

stumbled out of bed and put on some yoga pants and my old university t-shirt. I brushed my hair and teeth and added a small amount of makeup. With my dark hair, pale skin, and lack of sleep, I kind of had a "goth vampire girl look" going on.

Although the image of the perfect man was still looming in my mind, I went about my morning. I definitely needed some coffee. I locked my apartment and headed over to the coffee shop downstairs.

I lived in an apartment home community in the heart of Silicon Valley. I moved in about a week ago. They gave me this great price on a recently remodeled two-bedroom, two-bath. I had a bunch of furniture, so the extra space helped.

It was 9 AM. People were walking their dogs, jogging along the park, busy with their mobile devices — just a typical Saturday. It was beautiful outside; a clear day. The large palm trees were gently swaying in the wind. I picked up a cold foam cappuccino and parked myself at one of the tables under an umbrella. It was nice to be at peace after a series of unfortunate events over the last few years.

About three years ago, my husband of ten years filed for

divorce. We weren't able to have children, which led to communication issues. He accused me of being married to my career and possibly even having an affair. That was far from the truth, of course. However, in his mind, we were done. The only positive was the divorce settlement, which left me with a fair amount of savings. However, my father's failing health led to large medical bills, back taxes... I helped out as much as I could up until the end. My father lost his battle with cancer and advanced kidney disease. The bright side was that I had a stable job, close friends, and a sweet kitten at home to keep me company. I decided to take a month off from work, though, to sort things out in my head.

I took out my phone and began browsing through the headlines. Stocks, politics, latest celebrity gossip...wait, this seemed interesting: "Missing Girl, Ohio State University Campus — Jamie Patterson, 18..."

Before I could get to the story, a message came in. It was a text from my ex-husband, Rob.

"Alex, I'm sorry about your loss. Jim was a good man. I know this must be very tough for you. What I am about to say will not be easy, but here it is: I'm getting married again. I've known Melissa now for two years, and I feel it is the right time. We are also expecting a baby in June. This really comes as a pleasant surprise. I wanted for you to hear it from me first rather than just finding out second hand. Hope you are hanging in there."

Of course, this wasn't going to be easy for me; however, I had braced myself for this moment ever since Rob told me that Melissa moved in with him. I just stared at the text for about fifteen minutes. I figured I should reply back and feign happiness. Rob shattered my heart, more so than anyone ever could. I couldn't eat or sleep well for days. It was like a part of my soul had died.

Given my responsibilities as a caregiver, having romantic

relationships was difficult post-divorce. There were a few lovers and one-night stands — nothing significant. I was an idealist, always seeking the "perfect romance."

I thought I had the perfect romance with Rob. We met on a blind date. Rob was at an engineering conference that day, and I worked in tech support for one of the big internet giants. We opted to go bowling and then have dinner. I was actually a pretty good bowler; my dad taught my sister and me at a young age. Dad usually bowled 250+. He really should have gone pro, but his bad hip always caused problems for him.

"You're pretty good over there, shorty," Rob said as I hit a turkey. He just had to comment about my height. Being only 5 feet 2, I still could swing with the best of them. Unfortunately, Rob wasn't the best bowler; he had a number of gutter balls.

"See, software engineers aren't good at everything," I mused. Rob smiled back; he had such an amazing smile. He was the epitome of the phrase "tall, dark, and handsome." He totally made my heart melt.

We then had a wonderful dinner at the Chinese restaurant near the bowling alley. We talked for over two hours. It was refreshing to not only be attracted to someone but to also have a great conversation. I really hoped he liked me at that point. I got my answer as we left the restaurant.

"Hey, hold right here." Rob stopped me as we were walking back to my car, and he gave me a warm, gentle kiss. Poor guy had to bend down a bit to kiss me, as he was well over 6 feet. Who cares? I was in love.

"Shell! I met the man I am going to marry!" I shouted on the phone to my sister as I drove back home. And it happened, three years later.

———

I didn't have any family left in the area. Mom died shortly after Shell was born. Dad never remarried. In fact, he loved that quote from Betty White: "Once you had the best, who needs the rest?"

Our aunt Ada helped out a lot when we were growing up. She ended up retiring with her family in Florida. Last year, Shell moved to San Diego with her husband and the girls. So, after my divorce, it was pretty much just me and Dad.

Today was flower clean-up Saturday at the memorial park. Dad was laid to rest next to Mom at an outdoor mausoleum. I drove up the hill and had the replacement flowers with me.

Dad entrusted me with his care and arrangements. Once we had learned that his cancer had metastasized to his bones, Dad's health spiraled downward at lightning speed. I had to rush home from work to meet the in-home care nurse. EMTs were there to get Dad's heart starting again, and he was rushed to the emergency room.

"Are you Alexandra?" A man in his 50s with a strong European accent, German, perhaps, interrupted my thoughts as I sat in the emergency waiting room.

"Yes, I'm Alex."

"Alex, I'm Dr. Kraus. You are James Anderson's daughter? If you can follow me." Dr. Kraus guided me to the emergency room operating floor. They had Dad hooked up to so many machines. It was just so overwhelming.

"Alex, your father's potassium level was at 11. His kidneys failed. Unfortunately, there is nothing more we can do. He is 'brain dead.' You need to make the final call, Alex." Dr. Kraus paused to allow me to absorb what he said.

The choice was mine. Did I not do enough to help him? I felt so powerless. I couldn't save him. Hell, I couldn't even save my marriage. There was only one thing I could do. I looked over at Dad. It was time to just let him go so he could join Mom.

"Go ahead," I whispered to Dr. Kraus.

The rest of that moment was a blur as the nurses and Dr. Kraus ended life support for Dad.

"Beautiful day, isn't it?" A quirky female voice startled me as I was sitting on the bench in front of the family crypt.

"Oh, Rox! Sorry, I didn't see you there."

Rox was the funeral director who assisted in the interment. She was in her 40s, about my height, curvy with loud red hair. Ever since we bought the family crypt, she would call me to tell me about random "sales" for additional plots or crypt add-ons. In fact, she called me over Thanksgiving last year about their "Black Friday" sale. Well, I guess "death" was a business, too.

"I use flower clean-up day as a chance to check in with some of the families as well. How have you been, girl?" Rox asked as she touched my shoulder.

"Well, I'm hanging in there. Been a bit difficult to sleep, but that's to be expected, right?" I thought about mentioning my episode this morning, but I wasn't quite ready to talk about it.

"Oh, it happens a lot with traumatic episodes," Rox replied. "It will get better, though. Just takes time. I'll let you get back to your visit."

"Thanks, Rox," I said as she began to walk away. The flower cup holder was way up high. I needed the pole to help me reach the cup. "Hey, Rox!" I yelled, "Where's the p—?" Rox picked up a call as she was walking, so she didn't hear me shout out to her. I had to look around for it myself.

The mausoleum had three tunnels, all reserved. Guess these were nice commission checks for Rox. I referred to the people interred as my parents' "new neighbors" — Ashley Browning, a 16-year old who tragically died in a car accident; the DiMatos, ten crypts reserved for the large Italian family; Rebecca Eriksen, a 55-year old mother of three who lost her battle with ovarian cancer. Each plot had a marker with a photo. So many people with interesting life stories; tales of love, tragedy, joy, pain… I finally located the pole. It was next to *him*. Oh my God, it was the man in the still image. In fact, it was the *same image* from my dream: Dr. Scott Andrew Collier (March 3, 1982 — May 20, 2017),

"Forever in our hearts." My perfect dream man lived in the area? Dead at the young age of 35? I was fascinated.

"He was such a beautiful boy." An older woman, maybe around 65 years old, startled me with her heavy East Coast accent. She was about 5 feet 5 and wore a summer dress and a large hat.

"Oh, I'm sorry. I didn't see you there," I said politely. "Was Scott your son?"

"Scotty was my only child. Oh, I loved him so. He was so handsome, smart, and perfect." The woman proceeded to add new flowers to Scott's crypt.

"Ma'am, how did he die, if you don't mind me asking?" I inquired of my newfound friend.

"Scotty died in a car accident," the woman said as she gently arranged the flowers. "He was a research scientist and did such sophisticated things that blew my mind! Scotty went to Seattle one day to work on a special project. He was driving back to his hotel and lost control of his vehicle…

"Oh! I almost forgot…" The woman reached into her large Luis Vuitton handbag and pulled out a handmade woven object to hang over the flower vase.

"What is that?" I asked curiously.

"That, my dear, is a dream catcher," the woman said. "Scotty had these terrible nightmares; he always went to sleep with it. I couldn't find it until yesterday. Else, I would have placed it in his casket. Did you know Scotty?"

"Oh, no I did not." I wasn't about to tell her about my dream. "I just came over to grab this pole. My father is interred in this same mausoleum."

"Too bad; you seem like a sweet girl," the woman said with a smile. "Scotty never married; he never seemed to find 'the one.' He looked for her long and hard, but no one ever fit the bill.

"What is your name, dear? I'm Diane."

"My name is Alex," I said to the woman. "Well, Diane, I'll leave you be. Thank you for the chat."

I walked back to my dad's crypt. Hmm, Dr. Scott Andrew Collier, a brilliant scientist, never married, and died tragically. *How was I connected to all of this?*

PART TWO

BONDING

t was around 3 PM, and my friend Steph planned to stop by. Steph was 38 years old, had a Master's in Cognitive Psychology from UCLA, lived with her boyfriend Ryan, a firefighter, and had no children. She was tall, cute, and had dark, curly hair. Her father was Jamaican and her mother was Swedish. Steph worked at Stanford in the sleep clinic. We both went to Cal for undergrad in Psychology, but we didn't actually meet until about seven years ago when I used to do tech support at the Behavioral Sciences Center on the Stanford campus. At the clinic, Steph focused on mood disorders and how they affected sleep. We made it a point to meet up each week to talk through my sleep deprivation problems, in addition to the latest gossip.

While I waited for Steph, I did some searching online about my new obsession, Dr. Scott Collier. I found his public obituary on the memorial park website.

Scott Andrew Collier, PhD, an award-winning artificial intelligence research scientist, was born in Boston, Massachusetts to Timothy and Diane (Murphy) Collier. He was preceded in death by his father and two step-fathers (Douglas King and Adam Burgess). Scott had a large family: many aunts, uncles, and cousins. A scholar-athlete growing up in Boston, Scott was the state record holder in the 200-meter butterfly. He graduated from the prestigious Holy Cross Academy and then attended MIT, where he earned his BS, MS, and PhD. His research in robotics and AI led to numerous patents, even at a young age. His last known research centered on the concept of "the collective consciousness" and how it related to dreams. He moved to the San Francisco Bay Area shortly after receiving his doctorate to continue his research at various laboratories in the region and guest lectured at Stanford. Even with his successful career, Scott still made time to have a huge social circle. Friends described him as "handsome, charming, and overly generous." The funeral service will take place on May 27 at 10 AM.

Lectured at Stanford; I wondered if Steph knew who he was? My doorbell rang. I was still old-school and had to use the peephole to see who was at the door.

"Hey, Triple-A," a friendly voice sounded from the outside.

I hated it when Steph called me that. I earned that silly nickname because my full legal name was Alexandra Alice Anderson. When I married Rob, my initials stayed the same: his last name was Archer. Go figure.

Steph came in with a bottle of wine, cheese, and crackers — and she just couldn't wait to start talking. I loved that about her; she had a way to get me out of my shell.

Steph settled in on my love seat while Elmer, my kitten, raced off to the other room. I brought over a tray with the wine and snacks and then sat next to Steph.

"Hey, did you hear about that girl who is missing at Ohio State?" Steph asked as she poured me a glass of wine.

"Yeah, I was getting ready to read about that when 'you know who' sent me a text," I said as I took the glass from Steph.

"Oh, God. Rob. Was he gloating again about 'perfect' Melissa?" Steph rolled her eyes as she asked.

"Well, he's going to marry her, in fact!" I shouted as I took a sip of vino.

"O.M.G., no!" Steph's eyes were wide open.

"But that's not the best part," I said sarcastically. "She's pregnant!"

"Get out!" Steph yelled in surprise while spilling some wine on her blouse. I quickly ran to the kitchen to get a wet rag.

"Okay, okay, hold on here," Steph said as she gained her composure and cleaned herself off. "So, all of a sudden, Rob has miracle sperm? Oh my God. How are you holding up?"

"I'm okay," I assured her. "It was bound to happen. I just really need to move on."

I still had wedding photos, my wedding gown, my engagement ring, my wedding ring and a large number of cards and love letters from Rob. Maybe it was time to part ways and stop clinging to the past?

"Let's shelve that for a moment," I said. "I want to tell you about something very bizarre."

"Okay, I'm listening," Steph said with her mouth full of crackers.

"I had the weirdest thing happen to me last night," I continued. "Remember, I have been having problems sleeping? Well, I slept about five hours, but before I woke up, I saw these rapidly changing still images appear before my eyes."

"Parasomnias," Steph interrupted. "Not uncommon for people who have gone through all the trauma you have experienced."

"Okay, then, parasomnias," I said agreeably. "Well, there's more. The last image that appeared was of a man, about mid-30s, very handsome. I was totally drawn to him. But, get this, Steph, he was a real person! I saw his vault at the cemetery today; he's in the same mausoleum as my parents."

"Whoa! That's…that's pretty creepy!" Steph crinkled her eyebrows in disbelief.

"Seriously, his name is Scott Collier; he's a research—." Steph stopped me mid-sentence.

"Wait a minute. Alex, are you referring to Dr. Scott Collier, the research scientist from MIT?" I shook my head in agreement with Steph's question.

"He's been to my lab a lot. He died in a car crash. It was in the news." Steph gave me a "didn't you know this already" look.

"Steph, come on, you know how life has been for me the last few years," I explained. "I feel like I have had tunnel vision. I've only recently started keeping up with the latest events."

"Okay, let me get this straight." Steph always liked to recap. "You saw Scott in a hallucination. Then, you stumbled upon his grave today. And you had no idea who he was?"

I nodded in agreement.

"Coincidence?" Steph asked in hesitation.

"I don't know, Steph. What do you know about him?"

"Well, I didn't interact much with him, but I am familiar with his research," Steph went on to explain. "People were just in awe of him: brilliant, handsome, charming. I mean, I remember once he asked me where the men's room was located, and his 'thank you' smile alone was enough to make me weak in the knees. He was kinda mysterious, though. He was really fascinated with parasomnias. In fact, I recall that he claimed to have had some bad nightmares when he was a kid. I'd have to look back on our files."

"Yes!" I interrupted. "Actually, I met his mom at the cemetery. She added a dream catcher to his flower vase. So, looks like the nightmares were pretty serious."

"What was his mom like?" Steph asked. "You can tell a lot about a man from his mom."

"Um, well, she was 'interesting,' to say the least," I mused. "Her Louis bag, unless it was fake, indicated to me that she liked status. She kept gloating about how 'perfect' Scott was."

"Ehhh…" Steph interrupted. "Mama's boy. Probably has

narcissistic tendencies. Madonna-whore complex, too, like Trey MacDougal on *Sex & the City*." Steph started laughing.

"Geez, don't be so quick to judge, girl!" I jokingly yelled at Steph.

"Well, when I get back in the office next week, I'll let you know what I find," Steph added as she took another sip of wine. "Are you still keeping your sleep journal? Continue to do that, and, in the meantime, try to relax. We'll figure this out."

That was easy for Steph to say. I felt so unsettled.

———

The time was 10 PM. Elmer had been lounging on my bed ever since Steph arrived and decided to stay there when she left. I put on my pajamas and slipped under the covers. I wondered if the images would appear again tonight? Based on some internet searches, parasomnias were sporadic. There was no guarantee I would have these visions every night.

Well, it was hard to get to sleep, so I opted for the radio. Something I hadn't listened to in a while was *Things That Go Bump in the Night*, hosted by Pete Williams out of the high desert in Nevada. I had always been a fan of the paranormal, which I often felt was an extension of Psychology. Being an INFJ in the Myers-Briggs model, I was typically viewed as someone who had a psychic-level of intuition. So, I relaxed with my head-phones as Pete Williams took me to "dark places unknown."

"Thank you for joining us this Saturday evening, October 21, 2017. For tonight's show, we are going back to the topic of urban legends. Back on May 20, we focused on Bloody Mary. Tonight, we received a number of calls and emails claiming that missing Ohio State co-ed, Jamie Patterson, was 'taken' by the mirrored mistress."

Oh wow! That reminded me; I needed to follow up on that story.

"We're gathering more facts and will follow up as soon as we have a clearer picture. In the meantime, we will focus on another mysterious figure: The Fedora Man. This will be a wild tale for all you insomniacs out there…"

As Pete went into the origins of The Fedora Man, I started feeling really drowsy; kinda odd because I was so restless just a moment ago. Pete's voice faded as I went into dreamland.

I had been asleep for close to five hours when I felt myself coming out of the dream state and into wakefulness. It happened again: rapidly changing still images. I felt a little more aware this time.

"Slow down," I told the images.

They slowed down!

"Speed up," I told the images.

They sped up again.

Then, there he was, Scott Collier.

"Stop!" I said.

Scott's still image froze before my eyes. It was a different picture of Scott. He was wearing a business suit and a fedora. He still looked extremely handsome, but something was off.

"Hello," I said.

The image suddenly came to life!

"Help me, Alex," Scott said.

I instantly shot out of bed in terror! *He heard me and knew who I was!*

PART THREE

THE FEDORA MAN

At this point, I had no idea what was going on. Parasomnias. I'd heard something about this before on *Things That Go Bump in the Night*. The show had a user forum online. I decided to browse it for information: Encounters with Bigfoot, UFOs, Urban Legends, ahh ... Dreams. I opened the Dreams forum under the subtopic "Parasomnias." Seems there was quite a bit of activity recently.

Looks like "abigail_parker" posted on March 12, 2017:

"As I am beginning to wake up, I see a myriad of fast, still images flashing before my eyes, through my mind. I can often remember a lot of them, but can't seem to find any special meanings. This can go on for quite some time, intermittently between drifting in and out of regular non-REM sleep. When this happens I really can't wake up properly; I'm still very sleepy, and it feels that I should sleep it off. Anyone else experienced this?"

I added my reply; maybe Abigail would see it?

"This phenomenon has been happening to me, too — ever since my father passed away. One thing I have been able to do that I haven't seen anyone post yet: I have been able to TALK to the image. For example, one of the images was that of a young man in a hat. I told the still image to 'stop.' It stopped. Then I said, 'Hello.' The image 'came to life' and said, 'Help me, Alex.' I woke up in terror; shivering, had to catch my breath. It was so scary! Please, if any of you read this, contact me."

As I closed the lid of my laptop, I heard a knock on my door. It was 3:33 AM. Who would be knocking on my door this early? It was a gated community with onsite security, but sometimes people wandered in. I looked in the peephole; there was no one there, but there was a package left on my doorstep. I slowly opened the door; there was no one around. It was quiet, and the walkway was well-lit. On the ground was an open box with two items: a journal and a fedora, just like the one that Scott was wearing in the image! I quickly grabbed the box and locked my door immediately.

I didn't care what time it was, I needed to call Steph.

"Pick up, Steph…" I said to myself.

"Alex? It's, what, 3:45 in the morning? What is going on?" Steph asked while yawning.

"Steph! Someone randomly left a box at my front door. It has a journal and a fedora in it. This is really super creepy. And, on top of it, Scott *talked* to me in my dream while wearing this *same fedora* from the box! He said he needed help. Can you and Ryan *please* come over?"

"Girl, we're coming in thirty minutes. Don't touch anything."

I just sat on my couch frozen and stared at the mysterious items. *What in the world was going on?*

———

Steph, Ryan, and I sat in silence on my sofa for close to ten minutes.

"That is one funky Freddy Krueger-esque hat over there," Ryan commented and broke the silence. "You know that Freddy was based on 'The Fedora Man,' right?"

"Yes!" I added. "I fell asleep during last night's episode of *Things That Go Bump in the Night*. Pete was going to tell the story of 'The Fedora Man.'"

"Triple-A, we listened to it," Steph said. "A guy who has been doing some consulting with us, Dr. Paul Yang, was the guest speaker. Can you grab your laptop? The live stream should be archived."

Dr. Paul Yang graduated from Harvard and was one of the leaders in sleep disorder research. He was an average-sized man, mid-40s, Asian descent. He worked closely with Scott, and they were friends.

I opened my laptop and found the episode online. We skipped over to the interview with Paul:

Pete: "I am here on our guest speaker line with Dr. Paul Yang, who consults at the Stanford sleep clinic and specializes in parasomnias. Thank you, Dr. Yang, for joining the broadcast."

Paul: "No, *thank you* for having me."

Pete: "There's a lot of buzz out there that the scary stories we were told as kids are real. I mean, we are hearing word that Bloody Mary may be REAL. What are your thoughts on urban legends?"

Paul: "You remember Ed Warren? I am sure your audience knows who he is, but, if not, he and his wife were the paranormal researchers in the real Amityville Horror."

Pete: "Yes, absolutely."

Paul: "Well my favorite quote from Ed, paraphrased, is: 'The fairy tale is true. The devil exists. God exists. And for us, our very destiny hinges upon which one we elect to follow.' So, as a man of science, I take an agnostic approach. I work with a lot of patients who are struggling with horrific dreams, hallucinations, sleep paralysis... What they are experiencing is *real* to them. Maybe we should be keeping an open mind?"

Pete: "I like that approach, Doctor. Tonight, we are focusing on 'The Fedora Man' phenomena. Seems since around May, there has been a sharp increase in the number of reports globally of this mysterious figure that haunts people in their sleep. From what we gather, he feasts on fear. What's your take on this?"

Paul: "I have been speaking with a number of witnesses who claim to have interacted with 'The Fedora Man' in their dreams. He is apparently looking for his 'other half.' Seems he has 'consumed' a soul recently tainted with personal demons and emptiness; he now needs to find the ultimate compassionate soul to balance him out. Think of yin and yang; dualism. With this combined power, 'The Fedora Man' can manifest himself in and out of the dreamworld and freely roam the Earth!"

Pete: "God and the devil. Like Ed Warren said. My jaw is dropping! How can he be stopped?"

Paul: "Unfortunately, I don't know the answer. He's seeking an *empath*; someone who has deep intuition, almost psychic-level. That person is going to hold the key."

Steph closed my laptop.

"Okay, now that you heard the background story, there's more," Steph said with a serious tone.

"I'm listening," I said with a bit of hesitation.

"Well, after I left your place, I went back to work and

grabbed some files." Steph reached into her bag and pulled out some folders.

"Now, this is highly confidential. You did not hear this from me… Right, babe?" Steph looked over at Ryan.

"Uh, you were talking to me?" Ryan said with an innocent smile on his face as he was browsing his phone.

"See, this is why I love this guy," Steph said as she gave Ryan a quick kiss.

Steph continued. "Okay, you know those still images you saw? On March 12 of this year, Scott figured out a way to record these parasomnias visually. They are like reels of film; like a mini-movie. But, not everyone's can be recorded. It requires someone who has a deep connection into the collective consciousness. Scott had that special gift. He was able to record his own parasomnias. However, when he did this, he opened a gateway that allowed The Fedora Man to cross into our world. In his notes, he claims that there was a shadowy figure with a hat in his sample recordings.

"Given that you were able to control and even speak with these images tells me you might be that 'empath' that Paul was referring to on the show. I think The Fedora Man is looking for you!"

"Oh, that's really comforting," I said sarcastically. "There has to be a way to stop this."

"Well, let's take a look at these 'clues' you were given," Steph said. "Maybe you have a spiritual helper in all of this?"

I took out the journal. There seemed to be a lot of pages missing. On the inside cover it said, "This journal belongs to Abigail Parker." Abigail Parker from the online forum?

"Hey, I might know this girl," I said. "She posted on the *Things That Go Bump in the Night* forum about her own parasomnias."

"Well, let's give it a read," Steph demanded.

PART FOUR
ABIGAIL'S JOURNAL

March 13, 2017

Someone finally answered my ad for a roommate. I can't believe they increased my rent again. Even on a software developer's salary, it's been tough to stay afloat! Her name is Genevieve. She only wants to stay for three months. I can't be picky at this point; I need to pay the bills. She is really beautiful; tall, with long, dark brown hair. She likes wearing hats. She has a European accent. I think she is French, given her name. Anyhow, I am a total "Plain Jane" next to her; not even close to having model looks. She paid me cash upfront, which is a little odd…

March 27, 2017

Genevieve is gone a lot. She probably has some huge social circle. Speaking of "social," I signed up on a dating app. I don't know about these things. I like keeping to myself, but I need to "get out there." My friend at work told me that this app was the best. The first person to reply was a guy named Scott. He looks way out of my league. He is five years older, never married, no children. He has a freaking PhD from MIT! And he is gorgeous! I swear, if he saw Genevieve, he would probably drop me in a heartbeat for her. Apparently, though, he has little time to meet quality woman, so he's trying the dating app scene. He thinks I am pretty and wants to continue the conversation. I have his phone number, so let the texting begin!

April 14, 2017

I am so in love! I know I haven't met him yet, but I just have this feeling; a feeling of really connecting; it is so real. Scott feels it, too. Actually, he offered up that we may be soul mates. He's trying to set up our first date. It's just tough with his work and travel schedule. I know this seems lightning fast, but sometimes when you know, you just know.

April 18, 2017

We set it up! April 21 at 7 PM. We will meet at the bar downstairs at the Fairmont; then dinner at the nearby Italian restaurant; then "dot, dot, dot." OMG!

April 20, 2017

I caught Genevieve looking at my journal today. She said it was a mistake because she misplaced hers. Not sure I believe her. I will be locking this up each night.

Tomorrow is the big date! He sent me a text saying that he wishes we could just get married now and not tell anyone! He's obviously joking, but he is such a romantic. It's like two people who are so obsessed with each other and nothing else matters. Reminds me a lot of *Somewhere in Time*, when Richard connects with Elise, a romance that transcends beyond space and time. She knew he was coming; he would be her greatest romance or the one who would destroy her.

April 22, 2017

Last night was magical. We had so much chemistry. I spent the night with him at the hotel. I did learn something interesting: he used to have very bad nightmares. He kept a dream catcher with him. Something about a "man in a fedora" that haunted him since he was a kid? Anyhow, he says he loves me! I still can't believe it. He's going up to Marin next weekend. I'm going to see if I can go up there, too.

April 30, 2017

Scott said he would be at the house in Marin. I went up there; his car was there, but he wouldn't answer the door. I called, texted. Nothing. So I came back home.

Oh wait; a text just came in. He says he's sorry; he fell asleep. He promises to make it up to me. He says he has a room picked out just for us in Las Vegas. We just need to pick a date. I would love to spend the whole weekend with him.

Genevieve just walked in. Wonder where she was? I haven't seen her since Thursday.

May 15, 2017

He's been so distant. I think, though, by threatening to leave, I got through to him. He wrote me back today to say we can have dinner at Alexander's on May 18, as he is heading to Seattle for work on the 19th. I plan to confront him on his aloof behavior. He promises there is no one else.

May 19, 2017

Last night, I found him with another woman! I was late to the restaurant because my car wouldn't start. I had to do a ride-share. I finally got to the restaurant, and he was at the bar with some tall woman with blonde hair. She had something in her hand; I couldn't tell what it was. But she was laughing and so was he. I stormed out of the restaurant.

I can't believe I fell for this shit. He never really loved me. I knew he was either going to be my greatest love or my worst nightmare. I hate him. I can't breathe. I can't eat. I can't sleep. I left him so many messages; all ignored. I don't know where Genevieve is, but she left her sleeping pills behind, next to her fedora. It won't hurt to take a few, right?

Taped to the last page of the journal was this newspaper clipping:

Abigail Parker, 30, tragically passed away in her sleep on Saturday, May 20, 2017. She was the only child of John and Tessa Parker, both of San Jose. She attended San Jose State University, where she earned both her Bachelor's and Master's degrees in Computer Science. She was very bright and caring and will be sorely missed by her friends and family. Abigail wished to be cremated and have her remains scattered in San Francisco Bay.

PART FIVE
DREAMSCAPE

All three of us had tears rolling down our cheeks. Abigail was just an idealist looking for her perfect love and lost her life as a result — ironically, the same day Scott died in the car crash.

"God, why were you such an asshole, Scott?" Steph asked angrily as she looked up above, hoping Scott would hear her. "And this Genevieve character … She was as shady as hell. Betcha she caused Abigail to overdose!"

"Let's head down to the sleep center. I'm texting Paul to join us. He knows a lot about Scott's research. This is a matter of life and death."

"I'll bring the journal with me," I said. "What do you think about the fedora, Steph?"

"I don't know. Don't pick it up. Leave it in the box; we'll take it with us."

———

We drove in Ryan's car up to Palo Alto to the Stanford campus. Paul met us there and was able to get me cleared to enter the building. Ryan had to stay behind. Paul took Steph and I back to the lab where he stored the data and equipment from Scott's research. We showed the journal to Paul and explained the entire situation, including how I was able to control my parasomnias.

"Scott was like a brother to me," Paul explained. "It was very clear that he had commitment issues, but, you know, he did tell me that he met someone special, sometime back in April. I think he's referring to this Abigail girl. He saw her as someone who could give him unconditional love, unlike his mom."

"See, I told you. Mommy issues," Steph whispered jokingly to me.

Paul continued. "He was empty inside, just couldn't let anyone 'in.' Still, he was brilliant and passionate about his work. We have to get to the bottom of this, especially who this 'Genevieve' person is. I wonder if … nah, can't be…"

"What is it, Paul?" I asked.

"Could it be that Genevieve was really 'The Fedora Man?' I mean, think about it. Scott thought The Fedora Man may have crossed over to our world on March 12. Genevieve shows up on March 13. She loves to wear hats; comes in paying cash; only wants to be there for three months; invades Abigail's privacy and leaves her some 'pills?' All too convenient."

Steph and I completely agreed with Paul.

"Alex, you must be the 'empath' in all of this," Paul said as he looked at me sympathetically. "It's just a hunch, but I think Scott is trying to talk to us from the collective consciousness. He will reach out again. Let's get you set up."

I nodded in agreement. Paul had me go to the other room. I changed into a gown and rested in the bed. Steph came in and placed the sensors on my head and headphones in my ears. Calming nature sounds played in the background.

"Hang in there, Triple-A. We'll be monitoring everything; don't be afraid." Steph gave me a wink and went to the other room. I could see her and Paul through the glass.

"Okay, Alex, the machine is going to start up now," Paul said through a microphone as he turned on the equipment. "The still images have been appearing after you have been asleep for about five hours. These are technically referred to as 'hypnopompic hallucinations.' We will be recording this whole time. When you get to the hypnopompic state, what you are experiencing will appear like a movie on our screen. Again, this is surreal. Don't think about it; just relax and let yourself doze off naturally."

I was exhausted. My eyes felt heavy, and I found myself drifting off. It was going to take a while before the parasomnias would appear; in the meantime, Steph and Paul conducted some online investigations on Abigail and the mysterious "Genevieve."

"You know," Steph said. "Abigail lived in an apartment in San Jose; a two-bedroom. Hmmm…"

"What?" Paul asked.

"Yes! I knew it. Abigail Parker, last known address: The Commons, number 2187. That's Alex's address!"

"Energy is neither created nor destroyed," Paul interjected. "So, this means Abigail died in Alex's apartment. Her energy or life force may still be there. Being the empath that Alex is, she probably absorbed some of that energy from Abigail. It explains her instant attraction to Scott. This is all connected. What else was in the box that Alex found?"

"There is a fedora," Steph said. "It's similar to the one that people say The Fedora Man wears. I assume from the journal that this one belonged to Genevieve."

Steph lifted the fedora and found a note…

———

About five hours passed, and it happened again. The still images appeared before my eyes in rapid succession.

"Slow down," I said.

The images slowed. I carefully looked at each one until I could find Scott. Suddenly, an image appeared: it was a man and a woman at a restaurant. They were laughing at the bar. The woman was holding something in her hand. The man looked like Scott!

"Scott!" I shouted at the image.

He went from a still image to a real person. The woman remained as a still.

"Alex," Scott replied. "You came back."

This time I wasn't scared; I stayed in the dream.

"Scott, that woman next to you... What is her name?" I asked.

"She said it was Jen," Scott said. "It's her nickname; her real name is Genevieve."

Oh God, no. She died her hair blonde, and, from a distance, Abigail probably didn't recognize her.

"Scott, were you supposed to meet someone else there?" I asked.

"Yes," he replied. "A girl named Abigail. I call her Abby. I was supposed to meet her for dinner, but Jen started talking to me; I lost track of time. I haven't seen Abby at all."

"Scott, Jen is holding something in her hand. I can't see what it is. Can you describe it for me?"

"She is holding my dream catcher, Alex. We were talking about nightmares, and she wanted to see it."

"Scott, listen carefully, that woman next to you is not who you think she is..."

All of a sudden, Scott's image froze and the still image of the woman came to life. She then transformed into a shadow figure with a hat: The Fedora Man!

"You thought you were 'bonding' with Scott this whole time? No, it's been me; it's always been *me*," The Fedora Man said, menacingly. "You can't save his soul, Alex. He's empty and shallow. He thinks no one can possibly love him. Abigail was a threat. I could sense Scott's heart opening to her. I could not have that happen. His soul is *mine*.

"I seduced Scott as Genevieve and stole his dream catcher. He didn't have it with him when he went to Seattle. It made him so afraid; he could not sleep. Ahh, the taste of fear..." The Fedora Man paused.

"Sleepless without his precious dream catcher, Scott had a difficult time driving back to his hotel. He saw me standing in front of him on the road. He swerved into another lane and a speeding truck struck his car. He died instantly.

"And then sweet, innocent Abigail... You probably thought she overdosed on those 'sleeping pills' I left for her. She suffered from the same parasomnias as you, Alex. She saw a still image of Scott. She tried to reach him, but I stopped her. I fed on her fears; her fears of not being pretty enough, not being good enough ... She didn't die from the pills; I killed her in her sleep!

"You are next, Alex. Something is blocking me from tasting your fears. I will find out what that is..."

The images faded away, and I felt someone grab me.

"Alex! Alex! Wake up!" Steph shouted while shaking me.

"The Fedora Man," I whispered while attempting to catch my breath. "He's after me!"

"Alex, we saw the whole thing!" Steph said with urgency. "But, we might know how to defeat him! Scott left a note for Abigail. It was in the box under the fedora:

Abby, I have this unsettled feeling. Understand that I have a strong desire to protect you. I think I unleashed a monster. The only way to stop him from coming after you is for you to have this dream catcher. It has been blessed and contains the special protection you need. Please attach it to your bed-post. It will keep you safe. —Scott

"The Fedora Man stole Scott's dream catcher, so we think that this other dream catcher is the one that Scott's mom placed around Scott's flower vase at the mausoleum," Paul said as he rushed to take off my equipment.

"Come on, Alex," Steph said as she grabbed my belongings. "Ryan is waiting for us in the car. We're heading to the cemetery now!'

PART SIX
FAIRY TALES

"While you were asleep, Alex, I did some further reading on 'The Fedora Man' urban legend," Paul said while sitting in the front seat next to Ryan. Paul brought the fedora with him, and it sat on his lap.

"The Fedora Man currently can't walk the Earth on his own, so he may be in disguise. Similar to 'Genevieve,' he'll invade someone's body and take over. We have to be prepared for that. Don't trust anyone. We need to grab that dream catcher before he does. Remember, he feeds off of fear."

"Hey, this reminds me of *A Nightmare on Elm Street, Part 3*," Ryan said with conviction.

"Remember, Dokken, 'Dream Warriors!'" Ryan started singing in a cheesy tone and held up his right hand in a "devil horns" gesture.

"See why I love this guy?" Steph mused. We all chuckled.

———

We pulled up to the mausoleum. As we headed over to Scott's crypt, I saw Rox sitting on the bench nearby.

"Alex," Rox said. "I figured you'd stop by. I need to talk to you."

"Be careful, Alex," Paul warned in my ear as he walked past me. "Remember what I said in the car."

This whole situation was a little unnerving, but I was interested in what Rox had to say.

"We need to grab something. I didn't expect you to be here. So, what's going on, Rox?" I asked.

Before Rox could answer, Steph yelled, "Hey Alex! Paul found it! And, get this: no sign of The Fedora Man. We did it!" Steph and Ryan hugged.

"Wait, where's Paul?" Steph asked. "He was right behind us."

"So sure that The Fedora Man wasn't around? I think he's been here the whole time..." Paul slowly walked out from the entrance where Scott was laid to rest. He put on the fedora and had a menacing grin.

"Paul?" I asked in shock.

"See, you can't trust anyone, can you, Alex?" The Fedora Man took out Scott's dream catcher from Paul's jacket pocket. "Rest assured, Paul is okay; I'm just 'borrowing' him. I entered him when you and I finished that lovely chat in your head."

Ryan tried to knock down The Fedora Man, but he threw Ryan down with a simple push.

"Don't try to stop me. You all are weak and foolish. I have what I need, and I'll see you in your dreams, Alex."

A shadow figure flew out of Paul's body, taking the dream catcher and fedora with him. The figure and the items disappeared into thin air. Paul immediately dropped to the ground.

"Paul, Paul, are you ok?" We asked as we lifted him up.

"Yeah, what happened?" Paul asked as he grabbed his forehead. "The last thing I remember, we were watching Alex's dream on the screen."

"The Fedora Man took Scott's dream catcher, Paul!" I said in a panic. "What are we going to do next?"

"Nothing," Rox interjected. She opened up her handbag and took out something wrapped in tin foil.

"Here you go, Alex," Rox said with a smile.

I gave Rox a suspicious look and unwrapped the foil in front of everyone. The dream catcher … *Scott's dream catcher*.

"You had this all along?" I asked Rox. "So the one that The Fedora Man grabbed wasn't the real thing. How did you know this was going to happen?"

"Everyone, I have been in the 'death business' a long time," Rox said. "The fairy tale is true…"

Paul interrupted Rox, "The devil exists. God exists."

Then Rox and Paul said in unison, "And for us, as people, our very destiny hinges upon which one we elect to follow."

"Precisely," Rox said with a smirk.

EPILOGUE
LETTING GO

was able to break the lease at my apartment without penalty, as the property managers did not disclose that someone died there. I moved into Steph and Ryan's guest house in Mountain View. Elmer liked it better, as there were more places for him to hide. I made sure to use Scott's dream catcher every night to keep The Fedora Man at bay.

Determined to one day bring peace to Scott and Abigail's souls, Paul continued Scott's parasomnia research. Paul needed a lab partner, and I agreed to join his team at Stanford. Of course, Steph was excited about that. For me, it was just nice to be part of something that was greater than myself.

On the romantic front, Ryan introduced me to Mike, one of his firefighter co-workers (gotta love those men in uniform!). I also decided that it was time to let go of Rob. I went to the local thrift shop to donate my wedding gown.

Ed, the owner of the shop, played *Gossip Soup*, a pop culture "trash" show that streamed online, on the large television in the store. Host Sally Hyman went over the national headlines. I listened in as I browsed the store.

"Here are the headlines for October 31. Still no word on the whereabouts of Jamie Patterson, the co-ed from Ohio State, who has been missing since October 3. Jamie's boyfriend, Caltech student Mark Stevens, has started an online campaign claiming that a 'supernatural force' is responsible for Jamie's disappearance. *Things That Go Bump in the Night* host Pete Williams believes that someone opened a portal to another dimension that allowed 'Bloody Mary,' the childhood urban legend, to enter our world. Williams believes that this is just the beginning, and the worst is yet to come."

"Sounds all made up to me," Ed said with a snarky tone.

"Well, it is Halloween," I interjected. "Everyone's entitled to one good scare."

I finished browsing but noticed something on my way out: a dollhouse. The rooms looked so exquisite, such fine detail. The dolls inside were hand-crafted and beautiful.

"Pretty nice item for a thrift shop, huh?" Ed said.

"Yeah, any takers?" I asked.

"Actually, yes. We posted this online, and a person in Oklahoma City wants to buy it. We are shipping it out tomorrow."

"Great! Well, good luck to you all," I said as I walked out, turning my back to the dollhouse.

"Alex," a small voice whispered.

I turned around; there was no one there.

Oh, shit…

★★★★

*"Childish superstitions suddenly become fatally real.
The book delivers an entertainingly dark collection."*
— *Self-Publishing Review*

Dollhouse

JC BRATTON

DOLLHOUSE

★★★★

"Childish superstitions suddenly become fatally real. An entertainingly dark collection."
— *Self-Publishing Review*

DOLLHOUSE

"Aren't you a little old to be playing with dolls?" John's wife Myra was not impressed with his whimsical purchase. The elaborate, hand-crafted dollhouse from Japan came with three beautiful dolls, each one identified by name: Muffy, Buffy, and Duffy. Little did John know that each doll also came with her own chilling, macabre backstory, presented in a mysterious book sent along with the dollhouse. Fact or fiction? Unfortunately for John and Myra, they would soon find out...

PROLOGUE

his has got to be the greatest thing ever!" John channeled his inner geek as he took his big-ticket item out of its box.

"Aren't you a little old to be playing with *dolls*?" John's wife, Myra, didn't approve of his whimsical purchase.

"Come on, you know I love collecting." John brushed off Myra's comment. "From what the seller told me, this dollhouse was handcrafted in Japan back in the 1930s. Look at the architecture and exquisite detail. It's amazing. It comes with three dolls, furniture, lighting — the whole nine yards."

As John unwrapped the items from their packaging, Myra accidentally bumped into the shipping box and knocked it off the table. Something fell out of the box and slid across the floor.

"Hey, what's this?" Myra asked curiously. She brushed off the packing foam to reveal a book. It was hardcover, brown in color and looked quite old and worn.

John took the book from Myra. He quickly thumbed through the pages.

"It is handwritten, and the penmanship is beautiful — calligraphy. There are three ribbons bookmarking three sections, each one labeled with a name: Muffy, Buffy, and Duffy." John closed the book and then looked back at the dolls in their packaging. "I wonder…"

John unwrapped each doll to uncover that printed on the back label each of the dolls' dresses were their names: Muffy, Buffy, and Duffy.

"Okay, that is a bit creepy," Myra said in a shaky tone.

"Oh, come on; this isn't *Child's Play*. I'm sure it's nothing. In fact, I think it's rather cute; they're probably three sisters." John gave Myra a hug and kissed her forehead. "Just relax and help me move everything over to the den."

———

"I have a bit of a headache," Myra said as she rubbed her temples when entering the den. "The dishes are in the washer now. I think I am going to turn in early tonight. When are you coming to bed?"

John didn't pay attention to Myra; he was too focused on where to place the various pieces of furniture and how to strategically display the dolls.

"Earth to John…" Myra waved her hand across John's face to wake him up from his dollhouse trance.

"Oh, sorry, honey. What did you say?" John looked back at Myra.

"Never mind — just telling you I'm heading to bed," Myra muttered with an annoyed look on her face.

John got up from his chair and gave Myra a kiss.

"Aww, you know you will always be MY doll," John said apologetically.

"Don't stay up too late…" Myra headed upstairs to the bedroom as John sat back down and shifted focus back to his new obsession.

John took each of the dolls and lined them up in a row. There was something mystical about these dolls. Muffy had beautiful, flowing dark hair; Buffy was a natural beauty — she would be a model if she was real; and then there was Duffy — something was off about her. She wasn't as well-kept as the others. She looked a bit mischievous.

"Are you the bastard child, Duffy?" John snorted to himself.

The temperature seemed to drop suddenly after he said those words.

"Shoot, I bet I left the kitchen window open."

John walked into the kitchen and discovered that the window was, in fact, open, and it began to drizzle. There was a bottle of wine on the kitchen counter, so John decided to pour a glass and take a sip — or two, or three. After finishing the bottle, he proceeded to close the window; however, when looking outside, he could have sworn he saw someone — a woman wearing all white. John rubbed his eyes and looked out the window again; there was no one there.

"Okay, John, you had enough wine," he told himself.

When he got back to the den, he found the book that came with the dollhouse resting on his chair.

"Wait, how did the book land on my chair? Myra?" John questioned as he looked around the room.

Not one to be frightened easily, he picked it up from his chair, sat down and opened the book to the first page, which contained a string of Japanese characters.

花子さんの所有物

"Okay, not sure what that means," John whispered to himself. The rest of the book was in English, so he dived into the first section: *Muffy*…

PART ONE
MUFFY

never said that. Why do you keep making up stories?" Steve and Monica were at each other's throats constantly. Monica would call Steve a narcissist while Steve would complain that Monica was too sensitive. The two could go back and forth all night, especially when Steve had been drinking heavily.

They had two children: Ken, age seventeen, and Penny, age six. Penny was a complete angel in Ken's eyes: she had long, dark hair that was very soft to the touch. She was very kind and innocent. As Penny's big brother, Ken did his best to shield her from the Mom and Dad drama show.

"Daddy seems to hate Mommy," Penny said as she crawled under her covers.

"Hate is a strong word," Ken said to downplay the situation. "Sometimes grown-ups have disagreements. Don't be scared. Actually, I have something that will cheer you up…"

Ken opened up his backpack to reveal a beautiful doll with dark hair in an "okappa" style. She was wearing a Japanese kimono.

"Her name is Muffy. I bought her at a yard sale."

"I LOVE her!" Penny grabbed Muffy from Ken's hand and started to squeeze the doll very tightly.

"I knew you would like her." Seeing Penny smile was all Ken wanted.

"From what I understand, she was custom made by a brilliant Japanese artist. She put so much passion into her work. And it shows…"

"Muffy, you are going to be my best friend," Penny said as she looked Muffy in the eyes.

"Okay, I'll leave you to get to know your new best friend. I love you, kiddo." Ken kissed his sister good night.

"You are the best brother in the whole world!"

———

Over the next month, Penny and Muffy were inseparable. Penny would bring Muffy to school, have Muffy with her when she ate dinner, and would sleep with Muffy every night. Her parents were too wrapped up in their own perils to notice the profound change in Penny. She had a special friend that wouldn't judge her, that would always be there for her — someone she could take care of. Ken planned to go to college out of state next year, so knowing Penny had something to make her happy was all he could ask for… until Penny got sick.

Over the winter, Penny became very ill. The doctors did not understand what was wrong with her. Some sort of viral infection, maybe? She was in bed for weeks with Muffy by her side. One night, Penny became violently ill and started coughing up blood. She had to be taken to the hospital. When she got there, she awoke briefly only to find that Muffy was not there. With the chaos of trying to get Penny to the hospital, her parents forgot to bring Muffy.

"I need Muffy." Penny fought so hard to speak out loud.

"I'll bring her over; don't worry, kiddo," Ken assured Penny.

When Ken came back with Muffy, he was told that Penny had passed away.

Ken was in so much pain; he lost Penny, the sweet, innocent girl with beautiful long hair — the light of Ken's life. He sat in the hospital chapel and brought Muffy with him.

"Why did you have to take her from me?" Ken looked up and asked God.

Tears rolled down Ken's cheeks. He closed his eyes and just sat quietly. After about thirty minutes, he figured he should join the rest of the family. He grabbed his backpack and went to pick up Muffy — but she wasn't there.

"Wait, where's Muffy?" Ken pondered as he looked all over the chapel.

Steve and Monica found Ken in the chapel to let him know they were going to head back to the house.

"Have you seen Muffy?" Ken asked his parents.

"Muffy?" Steve questioned.

"Yes … Penny's doll…" Ken said.

"No, I'm afraid we haven't," Monica interjected. "Come on, Ken, let's go home and get some rest."

"Okay, well, let me look around some more, and I'll join you in a bit."

Ken asked the nurses, staff — anyone who could have possibly seen Muffy. No one had seen her.

"I *know* the doll was with me," Ken explained to the head nurse. "She was so important to Penny."

"We'll keep a lookout, Ken," said the RN in charge. "We'll call you right away when we find it. We know it's a difficult time for you and your family. Get some rest. If the doll is here, we'll find it and keep it safe."

———

Exhausted, Ken made it back to the house. His parents weren't home yet, which was a bit odd. He knew it would be painful, but the first room he needed to enter was Penny's room. The door was closed. Ken opened it and turned on the light to find Muffy in Penny's bed!

Suddenly, Muffy turned her head and looked straight at Ken. Her hair began to grow long like Penny's — right in front of Ken's eyes.

Ken was frozen; in shock.

"Will you be my new best friend?"

PART TWO
BUFFY

"You will *love* this place!" Mike and Amber's real estate agent, Kim Vu, gloated as she let them into the building. "It just came on the market. It's perfect for a professional young couple and probably the best condo you can find near Union Square."

Amber always wanted to live in San Francisco. Growing up in a conservative small town in Texas, she embraced the thought of being in a progressive city that was more in-line with her values. Mike, on the other hand, was born and raised in San Francisco. He had also lived in Tokyo for five years. He would have preferred it if Amber wanted to live in the countryside, like Napa wine country — something a bit slower-paced. But, he was too crazy about Amber to say no. They weren't married yet, and this would be their first time officially living together. When she passed, Mike's grandmother had left him with money for purchasing a home. This new place would be around the corner from his office, so he really couldn't complain.

The unit was on the top floor. The elevator opened, and Kim walked the couple to the condo's entrance.

"Oh my God, it's gorgeous! So much prettier than the

photos!" Amber was immediately drawn to the formal entry, French windows, hardwood floors, and vaulted ceiling.

"The kitchen is modern with stainless appliances, gas range, and dishwasher," Kim said as she guided the couple. "There is a circular private bedroom with a walk-in closet. The bathroom was updated last year, and this unit has a washer and dryer. I know not having that was one of the deal-breakers for you, Amber."

Amber was a bit of a "neat freak" and minimalist. Mike, on the other hand, never threw anything away.

"Hey, honey, check this out." Amber pointed out a secret curved closet with built-in shelves.

"Wow! What's this? A secret room?" Mike asked Kim.

"Kinda interesting, huh?" Kim responded. "The previous owner had this made. No particular explanation why, but it's definitely unusual."

Amber looked inside the closet and noticed a doll sitting on the top shelf, dressed in a kimono. It was very beautiful with a warm smile. There was something peculiar about the doll, though. She couldn't quite put her finger on it.

"Oh, don't worry about all the clutter," Kim said as she woke Amber from her trance. "The previous owner plans to have everything cleared out."

"Well, I am definitely excited about this place," Amber said as she held onto Mike. "What do you think, honey?"

Mike was lukewarm, but seeing the happiness on Amber's face, Mike didn't want to disappoint.

"Well, if this place makes you happy, let's seriously consider it," Mike said with a smile and kissed Amber.

———

"On move-in week? Seriously?" Amber was so frustrated when Mike called her with the news.

"I'm sorry, baby," Mike said apologetically. "There is an

emergency with a client in LA, and I need to fly out tonight. I'll be back on Monday."

The new condo was stacked with Mike's boxes. Mike finally promised to pare down on items after the couple watched a few episodes of *Hoarders*. However, much of what had to be unpacked belonged to Mike.

"Well, I am going to start organizing; I get the secret closet." Amber smirked as she tried to get over her disappointment.

"Of course! It's all yours. I'll call you when I get to LA." As Mike hung up on Amber, he couldn't help but to feel a bit unsettled. The natural protector in Mike was not happy that Amber would be by herself the first night at the new place.

———

About five hours had passed and Amber was able to get a lot done. The secret closet was almost to Amber's satisfaction; she was able to fill it with her ceramic cats, snow globes, travel items… After looking at the full closet, Amber mused to herself, "Wait, who is the real pack rat?"

As she unpacked the last box for the closet, the doorbell rang. Amber opened the door to find no one on the other side, except for a small box.

"Ugh, I'll bet it's one of Mike's boxes; must have left it downstairs," Amber thought aloud as she picked up the box and opened it.

"Oh my God!" To Amber's shock, the package contained a doll — the same doll that she had seen in the secret closet! In addition to the doll was a sealed envelope.

"What is all of this?"

Amber placed the doll on the kitchen counter and opened the envelope. There was a note with pasted letters and words from magazine clippings. The message was very clear:

If I cannot have you, no one can.

In addition to the letter was a photo of Mike and Amber, with Amber's face scratched out violently in red ink. Amber screamed in terror! She dropped the photo and ran to her phone to call Mike.

"Hello, you've reached Mike. I'm not able to come to the phone right now. Leave your name and number, and I'll get back with you as soon as I can."

"Mike, I need to talk to you; call me back as soon as possible."

Amber sent a text as well.

"Come on, Mike! Where are you?" Amber then looked at the clock; it was 7 PM. "Shoot, he's probably on the plane; he won't have access to calls or texts for about an hour."

Who would play such a sick joke? And why the doll? Amber looked back to the kitchen, and the doll was missing! Suddenly, chills travelled across Amber's body. She knew she wasn't alone.

"Amber..." It was a soft female voice, and it started giggling. "Come and find me!"

There was only one place she could be, Amber thought — the secret closet.

———

"Amber!" Mike shouted as he rushed into the condo. He took the first flight back from LA, as Amber was not returning his calls.

"Mike?" a soft voice said. "Come and find me."

"Amber?" Mike said hesitantly. The secret closet light was illuminated, and the voice sounded as if it was coming from there. Mike opened the closet to find a young, beautiful Japanese woman with dark hair and pale skin.

"Buffy!" Mike shouted in terror. "But...you're dead! You killed yourself the night we broke up."

"Shhhh…It doesn't matter anymore. We will be together forever."

"No!" Mike screamed.

Behind Buffy was a new doll on the toy shelf — it was Amber, dressed in a kimono.

PART THREE

DUFFY

"Hey, Pam, thanks for taking us in," Sam said while giving her a hug.

"Of course; you and Kimmie are welcome to stay as long as you want — this is your house, too," assured Pam.

"Thanks, but I don't hope to inconvenience you more than six months. Just need to get the insurance settled and the house repaired."

There had been a really bad storm. Sam's wife, Jill, was on her way home after a late shift at the hospital. Lightning struck a tree branch, and it fell on the driver's side of Jill's car, killing her instantly. Sam and Kimmie did not learn of Jill's death until the next morning, as the storm also produced a nocturnal tornado. Sam and Kimmie were able to stay safe in the storm cellar, but the house was badly damaged.

Sam had no family in the area. The only nearby relatives were Jill's. Pam was Jill's aunt, a widower in her late 60s. She owned a two-story home with three bedrooms, two bathrooms and an attic. Her husband had passed away ten years ago, before Kimmie was born.

At age seven, Kimmie had a general understanding of death.

She knew her mom was not coming back. She wasn't exhibiting any noticeable anxieties, but it was too soon to tell.

Kimmie was pretty quiet as she and Sam grabbed their belongings from the car. Pam noticed that Kimmie seemed down, so she thought of a way to cheer her up.

"Kimmie, did you know your mom had a special friend when she was around your age? Her name is Duffy. Want to meet her?"

Kimmie, still somber, nodded in agreement.

"What are you talking about, Pam?" Sam gave a questioning look.

"Didn't Jill ever tell you? When she was around Kimmie's age, she had a dollhouse. It was custom-made in Japan. Jill's father did a lot of traveling for work and picked it up in Osaka. There were at least four dolls at one point with the dollhouse, but over the years things get misplaced, thrown away… Duffy is the only remaining doll."

Pam, Sam, and Kimmie walked upstairs to Kimmie's new bedroom. Pam had anticipated gifting the dollhouse and Duffy to Kimmie, so it was all ready for her arrival.

Pam picked up Duffy and formally introduced her.

"Duffy, meet Kimmie. Kimmie, meet Duffy. I'm sure you'll become great friends."

Duffy was a porcelain doll wearing a kimono. She had some scars on her face, maybe from being played with a lot or just wear and tear over the years. Still, the doll seemed to bring a smile to Kimmie's face.

———

It was around 3:30 AM, and Kimmie was in bed with Duffy by her side. Kimmie felt something touch her hand. She slowly opened her eyes to see a woman with long, dark hair wearing a white gown. She looked a bit like Jill, but it was hard to tell in the dark. For some reason, Kimmie was not afraid.

"Mommy?" Kimmie asked.

"Shhh," the woman said, holding her index finger to her lips. "Come with me."

While holding onto Duffy, Kimmie followed the woman down the hall and up the stairs to the attic. The attic door was wide open.

Sam couldn't sleep. He watched some old videos of Jill. He missed her terribly. Suddenly, Sam thought he heard footsteps. He went to Kimmie's room to see her door was open, and that she wasn't there.

Worried, Sam shouted her name: "Kimmie!"

A horrific scream came from the attic. Sam raced up to the attic and froze in terror as he saw a girl *inside* a mirror in the attic. She grabbed Kimmie and pulled her into the mirror.

"Daddy!" Kimmie screamed as she tried to escape.

"Kimmie! No!" Sam was unable to move; a force stopped him in his tracks. Kimmie and the girl in the mirror vanished, leaving behind Duffy.

"Sam?" a woman's voice asked.

"Pam — it's Kimmie! She's gone!" Sam was able to move again and rushed over to the mirror.

As Sam looked in the mirror, he noticed that the woman behind him was not Pam. It was a woman with long dark hair and wearing a white gown. She was carrying Duffy.

"Sam, welcome to my dollhouse."

Sam turned around and screamed as he noticed that the person talking was not the woman in white; it was Duffy.

EPILOGUE

"Um, okay…" John said to himself in disbelief after he read the last page. "There is no freaking way any of that happened; these are *dolls*. This is a *dollhouse. It's not real*!

"Muffy, you are not Penny.

"Buffy, you are not Amber.

"And, Duffy … well, you already creep me out. But, nah… you are *just a doll*.

"And this is just a dollhouse crafted by some person in Japan. Get a grip, John. Just call up the guy you bought the dollhouse from in the morning and get this whole thing sorted. In the meantime…"

John placed each of the dolls in their rooms. He turned out the lights in the den.

———

"No freaking way…" John murmured to himself as he brushed his teeth and got ready for bed. It was 3:33 AM.

John entered the bedroom. It was dark, but the nightlight was on. Myra appeared to be sound asleep. He crawled under the covers and gently placed his arm around his wife. But, something was wrong. The woman next to him was not Myra. It was the woman in white with Japanese characters written in blood red across her gown:

花子さんの所有物
(Property of Hanako-San)

"Bloody Mary!" John gasped.

WHO'S BACK AT THE DOOR?

JC BRATTON

THE DIRECT SEQUEL TO THE BEST-SELLING YOUNG
ADULT SHORT STORY *WHO'S AT THE DOOR?*

WHO'S BACK AT THE DOOR?

★★★★

"A chilling tale and a well-crafted sequel to *Who's at the Door?*
Feeling like a supernatural horror movie on the page, this
scientific and paranormal mashup makes for truly fear-inducing
reading… effectively tapping into our collective fears of the
unseen world."
—Self-Publishing Review

———

WHO'S BACK AT THE DOOR?

After seven years of silence, Bloody Mary has returned. Jamie Patterson's disappearance became a cold case, and Mark Stevens, Jamie's boyfriend, decided it was finally time to move on; however, a member of sleep psychologist Dr. Paul Yang's team is brutally murdered and a chilling note is left behind. Investigators uncover video doorbell footage the night of the murder to find something shocking: Jamie was at the door...

PROLOGUE

The Ohio State University Campus
October 3, 2017

"So, Jamie and Mark got back together — again."

Shelly Patel rolled her eyes as she took a sip of her latte. Chatter filled a campus Starbucks, but Shelly and her friend Steve were still able to make conversation.

"I still don't understand what Jamie was so upset about. I mean, Mark is like *the* most devoted boyfriend *ever*." Shelly's tone was a bit somber.

"Do I sense a bit of jealousy?" Steve asked as he ate his croissant.

"No, no. Jamie is my girl. Chicks before di—" Before Shelly could complete her sentence, a loud crackle of thunder sounded.

"Shoot, I need to get back." Shelly jumped out of her chair and picked up her backpack.

"I'll see you tonight?" Shelly asked Steve.

"Of course!" Steve gave Shelly a warm smile as she headed out.

———

Shelly ran back to her North Campus dorm before it started to rain. She needed to get ready for rush events followed by a huge party at the Tri-Delta house. Steve acted as Shelly's "plus one," a role he played since high school. She hoped that Jamie would still be available, as it was critical for Shelly to get Jamie's opinion about the dress she planned to wear at the party. To make matters worse, her phone died, so she desperately needed her charger.

It was a little past 3:30 PM, and the dorm hallway was dimly lit. There were periodic rumbles from the thunderstorm brewing outside. As Shelly approached room 1138, something didn't seem right. The door was slightly open.

"That's odd," Shelly muttered. She then slowly pushed the door. "Jamie?"

There was someone in the room, but it was not Jamie. It was a woman with long dark hair covering her face and pale skin. She wore a white gown. The woman turned straight to Shelly and growled.

Shelly screamed in terror and ran as fast as she could down the hallway. The lights began to flicker, and Shelly could still hear the growling from the woman, as if she was following her. Not turning her back to see, Shelly quickly ran down the staircase and opened the door to the first floor. On the other side of the door was Tabitha, a Resident Advisor for the dorm.

"Help!" Shelly yelled. "She's after me!"

"Who? Who's after you?" Tabitha questioned and looked around and up the staircase. "Um, there is no one here. Look."

Panting, Shelly hesitated and then turned around to see an empty staircase. Suddenly, there were footsteps. Shelly screamed!

"Hey, I'm not that scary!" Tom Doyle, a Freshman, remarked in a sarcastic tone as he waved his hands up in the air and proceeded down the staircase.

"What is your name?" Tabitha asked.

"Shelly. Shelly Patel from room 1138."

"Okay, Shelly. What exactly happened?"

Shelly took a deep breath and explained the situation to Tabitha.

"I room with my friend Jamie. The door was slightly open, and I saw a woman with dark hair and a white gown. She began growling at me. It frightened me, and I ran down the stairs."

"You have no idea who this woman is?" Tabitha asked.

"Not in the slightest. Also, I didn't see Jamie. I hope she is okay! My phone is dead. I have no idea if she's been trying to call me." Shelly took out her phone and stared at a blank, lifeless screen.

"Well, Shelly, let's head to the campus police station and see if they can help."

———

"No, Mrs. Wilson," the male officer explained. "It's rush week. That naked boy in your yard wasn't trying to invade your home." Officer Julian couldn't help but snicker as she overheard her colleague on the phone. As the conversation continued, Shelly and Tabitha entered the office.

"Hey, Tabitha!" Officer Julian smiled as she recognized the RA. "What's going on?"

"My name is Shelly Patel," Shelly interjected before Tabitha could speak. "I live at Swift Tower, room 1138, with my roommate, Jamie Patterson. There was a strange woman who was in our room. She had long, dark hair and wore a white gown…"

Officer Julian's colleague immediately hung up the phone and gave Shelly an inquisitive look.

"A woman in white?" he asked. Shelly nodded nervously in agreement.

"I'm Officer Scott. So, your roommate's name is Jamie Patterson? Long dark hair? Her boyfriend is Mark Stevens?" Shelly and Tabitha looked at each other in amazement as Officer Scott spoke those words.

"I used to work for the County Sheriff. I had a, uh, mishap that involved Jamie and Mark this past summer. It led me to my 'demotion' and assignment here at campus police." Officer Scott rolled his eyes.

"So, can you help us, Officer Scott?" Shelly asked anxiously.

Officer Scott pulled up Shelly and Jamie's records on his computer.

"You're at Swift Tower? We have some surveillance cameras. Officer Julian can look through the last 24 hours of footage. While she does that, let's head back to the room. Who knows? Jamie may be back as well."

———

It was close to 6 PM, and the storm had passed. Shelly, Tabitha, and Officer Scott walked down the hallway to the dorm room. The door was wide open.

"Wait here," Officer Scott commanded. He walked through the suite, checked each door, looked under each bed, checked the lounge, the bathroom... no sign of anyone.

"Well?" Tabitha asked. "Is the coast clear?"

"Yeah, come in!" Officer Scott shouted.

Shelly found her charging cable and was able to glance at her messages. There was a text from Jamie at 3 PM:

Shell, I am heading to the library this afternoon. I hope to be back by 5.

"Oh no!" Shelly exclaimed. "Jamie's text says she should have been back by 5. It's 6 PM!"

Officer Scott's phone rang; it was Officer Julian. He placed her on speaker phone.

"Hey, Julian, what did you find?"

"Ummm — you've got to see this in person. You all should get back down here *now*!"

———

The group headed back to the campus police station and found Officer Julian studying the camera footage on her computer.

"Hey, this is super weird," Officer Julian explained. "As you can see here, at 3:33 PM, the door to room 1138 suddenly opens, as if on its own. Then, around 3:35, we see Shelly enter in and then run out of the room and down the hall — but then look what happens. Shelly, based on what you claimed, there should be a 'woman in white' following you. That's not the case."

"Oh my God!" Shelly shouted. "That's… that's Jamie!"

———

Clipping from *The Columbus Dispatch*, October 20, 2017

Information wanted on the whereabouts of Jamie Ann Patterson, 18, who has been missing since October 3rd. She was last seen leaving her dorm at Swift Tower on the OSU campus. Her roommate, Shelly Lynn Patel, 18, witnessed a mysterious woman present at the time Jamie was last seen. The only sign of potential vandalism was Ms. Patel's mirror; it was found with a large crack running diagonally through it…

CHAPTER 1

Present Day

J amie was gone. After seven years, Mark finally accepted that fact. Even with the video footage from Swift Tower, Shelly's testimony, and *everything* Mark had witnessed, the idea that "Bloody Mary," a childhood urban legend, was behind Jamie's disappearance didn't sit well with the authorities. In fact, the Waverly County Sheriff's office, the department that *knew* Bloody Mary was real, would not assist.

"This case is not in my jurisdiction, young Mark," Sheriff King said sympathetically. "I'm sorry that Miss Jamie is missing, but my hands are tied."

Even Jamie's parents were skeptical. With the video footage showing Jamie leaving on her own, and the fact that many young women go missing, they felt it had to have been an abduction. The local television show *Missing* released an episode on November 18, 2017, that discussed the "facts" of Jamie's disappearance and featured Mr. and Mrs. Patterson.

"Jamie is our baby." Mr. Patterson spoke directly to the camera while tears rolled down his face. "We... we need her back home safely. If you know *anything* about our Jamie, please contact the authorities. We *beg* of you."

There was no mention of Shelly's encounter with The Woman in White, and no one dared to bring up Bloody Mary.

Things That Go Bump in the Night radio and podcast host Pete Williams, however, suspected it was Bloody Mary all along. There had been an influx of supernatural or paranormal events since the death of Dr. Scott Collier, the scientist from MIT who may have inadvertently opened a portal to another dimension — one in which urban legends were real.

"Mark," Pete said in a serious tone over the phone one night. "I am receiving reports of very unusual phenomena: a man in a fedora haunting people in their sleep, a set of Japanese dolls that are possessed, mobile apps that know when you are going to die… yet, the authorities just want to bury this. When science and convention offer us no answers, might we not finally turn to the fantastic as a possible explanation?"

Rather than focusing on his schoolwork and internship with the Jet Propulsion Lab at Caltech, Mark spent most of his time chasing leads with Pete. It led to Mark's academic suspension after his Sophomore year. Although Mark's parents were not happy about him ignoring his college education, they did their best to support their son and helped fund his travels with Pete. But, after seven years of "wild goose chases," even Mark's parents had enough.

"Mark, we know how much Jamie meant to you, but it's really time to move on," Mark's mom said in a firm tone. "These 'investigations' with Pete *have to stop*. Look, we worked it out with Jamie's dad. He is willing to give you a job at Patterson AI. But, this 'Bloody Mary' business has to stop. *Now*."

Mark thought it over. Maybe they were all right; maybe it was just time to move on? Shelly worked at Patterson AI in the procurement department. She adjusted back to normalcy. In fact, she blew up at Mark about five years prior.

"Mark, I just can't anymore," Shelly said in a serious tone.

"Yes, I think I saw *something* in the dorm hallway that night, but I am sick and tired of you and Pete bugging me for more details. There is nothing more I can offer you. Please, Mark, move on or get some professional help."

Could Mark *really* move on? What else could he do? He lost his chance at Caltech, his friends thought he was crazy, and his parents were going to cut him off. He could move to Nevada and crash with Pete. But, for what result? Seven years and no sign of Jamie…

Mark sided with practicality. He took the offer from Jamie's dad. It was a full time engineering role with a great benefits package and stock in the company. A condition of his employment, however, was that he no longer stay in contact with Pete Williams.

"I'm sorry, Pete. It's time for me to just move on," Mark told Pete over the phone.

"But, Mark, we are so close! Dr. Paul Yang, the Silicon Valley parapsychologist, may have a lead for us —"

Mark interrupted Pete. "No! No, Pete. No more leads. I'm just done."

CHAPTER 2

Ross and Mary Montgomery moved to the San Francisco Bay Area shortly after Jamie's disappearance. Ross received a job offer to join a very prestigious Silicon Valley tech firm. Ross, however, would only take the opportunity if he felt Mary could also benefit.

Mary had no issue with moving. In fact, a lot had changed for her. She gained a sense of confidence that she didn't have prior. She grew out of her physically awkward phase and radiated with beauty, both inside and out. Her confidence was also reflected in her school work. She graduated from high school a whole year early. Mary attended UC Berkeley for undergrad and became fascinated with lucid dreaming and parasomnias. Her senior capstone project centered around the research of Dr. Scott Collier and how people may be able to manipulate their dreams.

Dr. Paul Yang, who ran a private sleep clinic in Silicon Valley, near the Stanford campus, was very impressed with Mary's research project. As a result, he invited her to intern with his team for the summer before graduate school commenced at Berkeley in the Fall.

"Oh my God, Mary! I'm so happy for you!" Ross gave Mary a gigantic hug when he read the letter from Dr. Yang.

"Thanks, Dad," Mary said with a smile. "I owe it all to you. Thank you for always believing in me."

"Of course," Ross said with encouragement. "Based on the letter, it looks like you'll have a new place to stay. You never got to experience living on your own. Are you sure you'll be okay with the transition?"

"Well, I just turned 21," Mary assured her dad. "I think it's time that I test the waters. I mean, it's just for the summer. How hard can that be?"

"Looks like you start next week! Wow! Maybe it's time I introduce you to your graduation present?" Ross gave Mary a half-smirk as he led her to the garage...

———

Mary's graduation gift was an all-electric Ioniq. This car aligned perfectly with Mary's values. She wanted not only to help people but also the planet. Mary packed up a few necessities and headed toward the Stanford campus.

It wasn't clear where Mary would be staying. The letter only mentioned "near the Stanford campus." Mary opted to head straight to the sleep clinic and would worry about the details of her stay later.

The sleep clinic had a classic Silicon Valley feel; it reeked of innovation. The windows were large — tons of light — an open architecture that looked unfinished but full of style. Mary entered the reception area only to be immediately greeted by Dr. Paul Yang.

"Mary. Mary Montgomery! I am so excited you decided to intern with us!" Dr. Yang said enthusiastically.

"Oh you cannot believe how thrilled I am, Dr. Yang!" Mary exclaimed. "I decided to drive straight here to the lab rather than to the apartment—"

"First off, call me Paul," Dr. Yang interjected. "And second, did Alex not tell you? You will be living in a gorgeous, recently renovated house! We have some houses that have been allocated to our visiting scholars, and you, dear, are a V.I.P. Let me send a quick text to Alex. You know Alex Anderson, right?"

Mary saw from the clinic's website that she was on the staff as Paul's assistant, but she knew little about her.

"Well, I know *of* her, but I have not met her formally," Mary replied.

"Let me text her now. I was out of town last week, and she was supposed to send you the housing details. Normally Alex is very prompt, so I am not sure why you didn't receive this information with your letter." Paul typed quickly on his mobile phone. "Okay, text sent! Let's get your badge, and then I'll show you where I need your help first."

Paul swiped his badge and opened the big glass door entrance into the main part of the lab.

———

Mary's first task, unfortunately, wasn't one she hoped. Paul assigned her to help sort and file a bunch of papers that came from Dr. Scott Collier's lab at MIT. The boxes sat in the lab for years, but Paul never had the time or patience to go through them all. All the boxes were moved to the third floor — a dimly-lit part of the building in stark contrast to the rest of the modern architecture.

Mary let out a sigh. "Oh well, Mary, all great researchers have to start somewhere." She opened room number three and turned on the light.

The room contained a desk, a chair, some supplies, a filing cabinet, and a laptop. There were at least 50 boxes stacked in the corner; however, one was set aside from the pack. The label on the box read *May 2017*.

"Oh wow, Dr. Collier died that month," Mary said to herself. As a result, the box piqued Mary's curiosity. Mary took a box cutter from the desk and opened it. Large stacks of manila folders filled the box. Maybe something ground-breaking would appear? To Mary's disappointment, folder number one read "Receipts." Mary let out a big sigh, but, as any other eager intern would do, she continued onward.

"This is going to take a while," Mary muttered to herself.

She began organizing each folder into the filing cabinet per Paul's instructions...

CHAPTER 3

A benefit of working on Dr. Yang's team was rent-free living in a gorgeous home near the Stanford campus. Alex Anderson did not take advantage of this perk until recently. She lived with her friend Steph in Mountain View, but then Steph had to move to North Carolina to take care of her elderly mother after her father passed away from Covid. Alex moved into the split-level home only a few weeks prior. The bottom level was to be occupied by Paul's new intern, Mary Montgomery.

As Paul's assistant, Alex had to get the house prepped for Mary's arrival. She also needed to send a message to Mary with the details of her stay.

A visiting scholar from Ohio State occupied the lower level for a few months and left behind a bunch of items, most of which were going to be donated. Alex had a lot of tidying up to do. In addition, a specific request came from Paul himself. He wanted a video doorbell installed as an extra security measure.

"Hey, I have absolutely no idea how to install this thing," Alex confessed to her boyfriend, Mike.

"What? You mean the doorbell camera?" Mike asked. "Come

on, it's a piece of cake! Leave it to me." Mike took out the parts and started assembling the device.

Mike and Alex had been dating on-and-off for the last seven years. After break-up number ten, they seemed to finally get on the same page. Mike planned on crashing a few days a week at the house, although, technically, Alex wasn't allowed to have sleep-over guests due to some line item in the 50-page contract she had to sign. This was the last day Alex would see Mike for at least a few days, as he was slated to work some long shifts at the fire station.

"Oh, shoot. I missed last night's episode of *Things That Go Bump in the Night*, and it featured Paul. I'm going to listen to it, okay, Mike?" Mike didn't even hear Alex, as he was hyper-focused on the installation. Alex put on her headphones and loaded up the latest podcast episode as she began sorting through the first pile of items to be donated.

Pete: Welcome to Things That Go Bump in the Night. Pete Williams here coming to you from the high desert in Nevada. Tonight we have a special guest. It's Dr. Paul Yang, world renowned psychologist and parapsychology enthusiast. Gosh, Dr. Yang, it's been, what, seven years since you appeared on the program? How are you?

Dr. Yang: I'm well, Pete. Very well.

Pete: Good to hear. Doctor, from what I gather you left Stanford to start your own clinic. How has that been going?

Dr. Yang: Very good, Pete. Let me first say that I have no ill-will towards Stanford; they were very supportive. However, I really wanted to branch out to areas that, let's just say, are unconventional. So, it was best for me to separate from Stanford and seek private funding.

Pete: And that's where Patterson AI came in?

Dr. Yang: Exactly. Allan Patterson, the brilliant robotics engineer-turned-entrepreneur, has become heavily interested in sleep and the research of the late Dr. Scott Collier — may he rest in peace.

Pete: I am curious, Dr. Yang, do you know what really happened to Dr. Collier that night in Seattle?

Dr. Yang: Umm, not sure why I am being asked this, but we all know that Scott died in a car accident...

Pete: I hate to tell you, Dr. Yang, but that's not the case. Scott was murdered. And you know the murderer, don't you — ALEX...

Pete Williams's tone changed. It was an eery cackle. It was the man in the fedora!

"No!" Alex screamed.

"Alex, babe! I think you're having a nightmare." Mike reached over to wake Alex, as she appeared to have fallen asleep on the sofa. She held a small package in her hand. Mike moved the package onto the coffee table and sat next to her.

"Mike! It's the man in the fedora... he's *back!*" Alex trembled.

"It was just a dream, Alex. What were you listening to anyway?" Mike looked over at her phone and saw the program name on the screen. *"Things That Go Bump in the Night*? You really need to stop listening to that show."

"Seriously, listen to the episode!" Alex changed her audio source to speaker and began playing the episode for Mike.

Pete: Haha! I'm glad you still have your sense of humor, Dr. Yang. I wish you all the best in your research. We'll be back in a moment and will take your calls for Open Line Friday.

"Umm, what was I supposed to hear? That's just Pete Williams…" Mike gave a perplexed look.

"But, that's not…" Alex felt a bit embarrassed. "God, I guess it really was just a nightmare. How long was I out?" Alex asked.

"Well, long enough to have a video doorbell installed! Take a look." Mike tried to lighten the mood. He and Alex walked over to the front door to see the new video doorbell installed and ready to go.

"You're a life saver!" Alex gave Mike a hug and a kiss.

"It's what I do!" Mike winked. "I left the instructions on how to install the app and complete the configuration on the kitchen counter." Mike looked at his watch. "Ouch! It's 3:30 AM. I have to head to the station now — late shift awaits!"

Alex watched Mike as he entered his car and drove off. She couldn't shake the nightmare. Something didn't seem right. Alex closed the door and proceeded back to the living room. She noticed the package on the coffee table.

"Okay, Alex. No more urban legends. Back to reality — and junk sorting." She let out a big sigh and grabbed the package.

Before Alex could open the package, she heard the doorbell ring. Maybe it was Mike? Alex walked to the door and opened it immediately. No one was there.

Alex then heard a woman's voice. It was muffled and seemed to say, "Help." Alex left the door open and walked over to the sofa. The package and her phone were where she left them. Alex listened carefully and heard the woman's voice again, but it was much louder this time: "Help!" It came from inside one of the boxes — a long box that had the word "mirror" written in red!

"What in the world is happening?" Alex asked herself as she opened the box. She uncovered a mirror with a large crack running diagonally through it. The reflection was not Alex; it was the reflection of a young woman located in what appeared to be a college dorm room. The woman looked familiar.

"Jamie? Jamie Patterson?" Alex asked as her heart raced rapidly.

"Look out! She's right behind you!" Jamie yelled back at Alex. Alex turned around to see a woman with long hair covering her face. She wore a white gown and stared coldly at Alex from the open front door...

CHAPTER 4

t was 3:33 PM, and Dr. Yang grew increasingly concerned as he had not heard from Alex after he sent the text message in the morning. He left Mary to sort Dr. Collier's old files, which would take some time. So, he decided to pay Alex a visit.

"Alex, this is Paul," he said over the car's speaker phone. "I haven't heard from you. I am a bit worried. I am heading over to the guest house now. Please call me back as soon as you get this message."

Paul also tried to get in touch with Alex's boyfriend, but his phone went straight to voicemail. There was a massive wildfire that struck Southern California, and a number of firefighters in the San Francisco Bay Area were called in to help. Paul suspected that may be why Mike couldn't be reached.

As he pulled into the driveway, Paul saw Alex's car. This made him even more uncomfortable. Could Alex be incapacitated? He immediately ran out of his car and to the front door. The door was unlocked.

"Alex?! Alex, it's Paul!"

Paul entered the home to find items scattered all over the living room; boxes were opened and the contents poured out as if *someone* entered the home with the intention of finding *something specific*. He then heard some rustling near one of the boxes.

Mee—row!!

"Good God!" Paul shouted as he placed his hand near is heart. It was Elmer, Alex's cat. Paul shook off the momentary scare. As Elmer darted off, something fell off the coffee table: it was a small package that was partially opened. Paul removed the rest of the packaging to uncover a Japanese doll dressed in a kimono.

"Odd..." Paul said in wonder. He placed the doll onto the coffee table when he noticed another peculiar object. It was a mirror with a large diagonal crack. The mirror's glass looked cloudy, so he could barely make out his own reflection. There was something written on the mirror in blood red: *Bring me Mary.* Paul gasped!

His phone buzzed. It was an unknown number. Breathing heavily, he proceeded to answer.

"Hello?" Paul asked in hesitation.

A muffled voice sounded on the other end. "Bring. Me. Mary."

"Who is this? What did you do to Alex?" Paul asked urgently.

"Upstairs bedroom," the voice muttered. The caller hung up.

Paul ran up the stairs to enter the top level where Alex resided. The bedroom door was slightly open. There was a foul odor coming from the bedroom. Paul opened the door and found Alex's lifeless body stretched out on the bed.

Paul closed his eyes, covered his mouth, and then turned his head briefly. Who could have done something like this? He opened his eyes and turned back to the horrific scene. Paul discovered that there was a message written on the wall near Alex's dreamcatcher, which hung directly above the bed's headboard. It appeared that the message was written using Alex's blood!

BRING ME MARY...

———

An hour had past, and Mary finally reached the bottom of the first box only to find a random thumb drive.

"Oh, God. Don't tell me that all these files were digitized…" Mary rolled her eyes as she picked up the device.

Mary walked over to the desk and sat down. She inserted the thumb drive into the laptop; the login credentials to the laptop were on a Post-It note attached next to the trackpad.

Mary opened the folder that appeared when the thumb drive loaded. There was one file with the name "SAC_052017.mp4." Mary opened the file. It was a movie — Dr. Scott Collier in a self-recording from a car at night.

My name is Dr. Scott Andrew Collier. I am a research scientist. It's Saturday, May 20, 2017 at 3:33 AM.

I think — I mean, I know I unleashed pure evil.

Scott sighed and looked away from the screen. Tears began to roll down his face.

I am a man of science. I wouldn't be saying any of this if I didn't witness it with my own eyes…

Back in March, I created a device that can record dreams. It was so amazing; I was able to watch everything that I dreamt the night before: vibrant colors; loved ones lost; exotic locations…

However, what I didn't notice until today was that the final scene of each recording contained a mirror in the background. And, in the mirror was a woman staring coldly at me. She had long, dark hair covering her face and wore a white gown. I believe this woman is known in the Eastern world as Hanako-san. In the West, she's known as Bloody Mary.

*In the final recording from May 17th, she left a note on the
mirror, written in blood. It said, "Bring me Mary."*

Mary suddenly had a flashback to when she was 13 years old —
to the day she saw a mysterious young girl with a teddy bear appear
in the restroom mirror — and to the day she saw a woman in white
at the cemetery. Mary went missing for a few weeks around the
same time period; she could never recall what happened. The local
Sheriff's department claimed that Mary was abducted by a cult that
released her without any explanation. None of it added up, but Ross
went along with the story. Mary had no reason *not* to believe Ross.
Mary just assumed everyone was telling her the truth — *until now*.
Scott's video continued.

*I have had no sleep. I lost my dreamcatcher the other night. But,
I need to get back to my hotel. There's a lot more to discuss. I'll
continue recording as I drive.*

Scott started up the car, placed his phone on a mount, and
began to drive. Before Scott could speak, there was a loud crash,
and the video became jumbled. The recording ended.

"Oh my God!" Mary shouted. "This was the night Dr. Collier
died! I need to talk to Paul."

Before Mary closed the file, she noticed something at the end
of the recording. She replayed the last scene before the crash and
slowed down the frames. About 10 seconds before the crash,
there she was. It was a woman with long, dark hair covering her
face staring coldly at the screen.

"Bloody Mary!" Mary gasped. She grabbed her backpack and
placed the thumb drive into one of the zip pouches. She ran from
the small office to the elevator. The elevator stalled, so Mary
rushed down the emergency staircase instead and found the
main entrance. It was close to 6 PM; the receptionist was ready to
leave for the day.

"Excuse me!" Mary shouted to the receptionist. "Where can I find Dr. Yang?"

The receptionist was a bit startled. "He went out to find Alex — Alex Anderson."

"Can I have the address?" Mary asked.

———

Mary drove to the address that the receptionist provided. There were a number of police cars and an ambulance. Mary parked along the street and jumped out of her car. She ran over to the front door but was stopped by the paramedics as they carted out a body from the house. She saw Paul inside talking to one of the paramedics. A young police officer proceeded to the front door, and Mary stopped her.

"May I ask what's going on?" Mary asked the officer.

"Are you a family member of the victim?" the officer asked.

Before Mary could answer, Paul appeared in the doorway and interjected. "Mary, you can't be here. Something terrible happened to Alex, but this is not the time to talk."

"But, Paul…" Mary pleaded. "It's about Dr. Collier — and *Bloody Mary*!" She took the thumb drive out of her backpack and showed it to Paul.

"Where did you find that?" Paul's face grew pale as he asked the question.

"I found it in a box marked *May 2017*. It was a recording from the night Dr. Collier died—"

"Mary, come with me." Paul grabbed Mary's arm and walked with her toward her car so they could have some privacy. "What's this talk about Scott and 'Bloody Mary?'"

"The thumb drive contains a recording from Dr. Collier the night he died. He said he unleashed 'pure evil.' And, Paul, I *saw her* — Bloody Mary. She was in the back seat of Dr. Collier's car—"

Before Mary could continue, a burly man, around 40 years old, approached Mary and Paul.

"Did I hear someone say 'Bloody Mary?'" the man asked.

Paul and Mary didn't know what to say. The man sensed hesitation so he introduced himself.

"I'm Adam. Adam Scott, Homicide Department." Detective Scott displayed his badge. "What are your names?"

"I am Dr. Paul Yang. I own this house. This is my company's newest intern, Mary Montgomery. She was scheduled to move into the house today."

"Wait, Mary Montgomery of Edenvale, Ohio?" Detective Scott said in shock.

"Umm, yes; how did you know that?" Mary asked with a confused look.

"I was a deputy assigned to your missing persons case," Detective Scott explained. "It's a long story, but I moved out here to the Bay Area as the money and benefits were *much better*. Besides, between us, I *cannot wait* to retire! I get a full pension!

"Anyway, enough of the small talk," Detective Scott continued in a serious tone. "Tell me what happened, Dr. Yang."

"Just call me Paul, please," Paul said and then explained the events that led to the discovery of Alex's body.

"I hadn't heard from Alex. She was one of the most reliable people I know. When I got to the house, it was a complete mess. I received a mysterious phone call from an unknown number that said, 'Bring me Mary.'"

Mary gasped!

"What is it?" Detective Scott asked urgently.

"Paul, that's what Dr. Collier said that was on the mirror. It said, 'Bring me Mary.'"

"Mirror, what mirror, Mary?" Paul asked.

"From Dr. Collier's dreams!" Mary added.

"Okay, let's back up here… Who is 'Dr. Collier?' And what about this 'mirror' and 'dream?'" Detective Scott was lost at this point.

Before Mary or Paul could answer, Henry, from Detective Scott's forensics team, ran from inside the house and interrupted the group's conversation. "Detective Scott! We have camera footage!"

Paul, Mary, Henry, and Detective Scott entered the house and walked to the kitchen table, where Henry had set up his equipment.

Henry sat down and guided the team through his discovery.

"Seems there was a doorbell camera installed. The username and password details were left behind on the kitchen countertop. It was set up to store recordings in the cloud. It only captured a few minutes, however, as the battery wasn't fully charged, and there was no audio."

Henry played the video clip. It showed Mike leaving the house and Alex closing the door.

"That's Mike, Alex's boyfriend," Paul confirmed.

Then, about three minutes later, 3:33 AM, it showed Alex opening the door and realizing that there was no one there. Alex walked back into the house and left the door open. Then, a figure walked up to the door. It was a woman wearing jeans and a sweatshirt. She had long, dark hair.

Detective Scott gasped!

"Who is that?" Paul asked.

"It's Jamie. Jamie Patterson…" Detective Scott replied in shock.

CHAPTER 5

Mark took a deep breath as he entered a conference room filled with some of the most brilliant minds in machine learning. It was his first week at Patterson AI, and the engineering managers were already impressed with Mark's ability to decipher complex algorithms. He was a problem solver and could always get to the root cause of an issue.

Shelly learned of Mark's joining the company and immediately buried all her ill-will. It was obvious to most that Shelly had a massive crush on Mark, ever since high school. Her loyalty to Jamie, however, kept her feelings in check. Now that Mark seemed to have moved on, Shelly felt that maybe it was her chance.

As soon as his meeting ended, Mark found Shelly waiting anxiously outside the conference room. He gave her a warm smile. It was nice to see his old friend again.

"Hey, wanna grab lunch today?" Shelly asked eagerly.

"Sure, Shell. Let me first catch up on some messages, and I'll join you in the cafeteria. Give me like, ten minutes."

Shelly nodded and headed out to the cafeteria.

Patterson AI had an open floor plan — no partitions; lots of room for collaboration. It was a casual-dress environment and had a "Silicon Valley"-feel to it. There were game rooms, lounges with televisions, tons of snacks — a really great atmosphere. Many of the engineers were heads-down with noise-cancelling headphones. They were all so passionate about what they were trying to accomplish. Mark sat down at his desk space, which was equipped with four large interconnected monitors, transparent displays, and random robotic gadgets — the casual observer could equate it to comic book hero Tony Stark's lab.

The company had been in business for close to 30 years. It pivoted over the course of the last few years to focus heavily on personal assistant technology that could *relate* to you; a digital "best friend," if you will. The company went public in 2019. It had an unprecedented IPO, which gave Allan Patterson the funds to expand and invest in areas that interested him. As a result, Mr. Patterson created a top-secret division, PattersonX. He invested in a number of start-ups that focused on sleep and consciousness studies. Rumor had it that they were close to solving the "mind-body problem." Mr. Patterson's obsession in this area had been criticized by investors, but this was personal for him. He lost his daughter; if there was even a remote chance that consciousness continued beyond death, it would help him and his wife, Jenny, to cope.

Mark looked at his phone, and there were 15 messages from Pete Williams. The first message read:

We need to talk. Urgent.

How many times did Pete send a message like that since Jamie's disappearance? 100 times? Mark hit the "Block This Sender" button and deleted the remaining messages without reading them.

"It's time to start your new life," Mark thought to himself. He placed his phone and laptop into his backpack and headed over to the cafeteria.

Mark grabbed a sandwich and soda and walked over to Shelly. Shelly wore an OSU hoodie and some jeans. She had her long, dark hair tied in a pony tail. Mark didn't realize until just now how pretty she was. She gave Mark the biggest smile as he sat down across from her at a small table.

"So how do you like it here so far?" Shelly asked between bites of her salad.

"Yeah, it's great!" Mark said with genuine enthusiasm. "The people are all very nice, and they are having me work on some really cool projects."

"That's awesome! You can see why people have been calling this place the *Midwest Google.*" Shelly continued the small talk. "Are you going to work on your Bachelor's degree?"

"Yeah," Mark replied. "There is a fast track BS/MS program through OSU that I am looking into. I just need about six months here to get the education assistance for it. It's really great. I feel I can get back on track, you know."

"That's so awesome, Mark!" Shelly replied.

Shelly took a deep breath and then spoke gently: "I hope this isn't too personal, but how are you coping? I know a while back I kinda got angry at you—"

"No, it's okay, Shell," Mark interrupted. "You were right. All those 'wild goose chases' had to stop. *We* know who took Jamie, but she's been quiet for seven years. I can't put my life on hold anymore." Mark reached out and held Shelly's left hand. "I'm ready to move on. I think Jamie would have wanted that..."

Before Mark could continue, a man in a lab coat interrupted the moment. He wore a Patterson AI consultant badge. It was Dr. Paul Yang.

"Mark Stevens, I'm Dr. Paul Yang. I need to talk with you — in private." He looked over at Shelly as he spoke the last word.

"Dr. Paul Yang, the parapsychologist?" Mark asked.

"Yes, Patterson AI is one of the main investors of my lab in Palo Alto, California. I am working on an initiative at PattersonX in which I need your assistance."

Mark looked at Shelly, and she gave him a shrug.

"Okay, let's grab a conference room," Mark said as he stood up and headed off with Paul.

———

Mark led Paul to a small, sound-proof phone room where they could talk in private and shut the door. There were two chairs and a small desk. Mark and Paul sat down and faced each other.

Before Paul could speak, Mark interjected firmly: "Look, I know you are friends with Pete Williams from *Things That Go Bump in the Night*. I already told Pete; I'm done. There have been hundreds of 'Jamie sightings' and none of them have panned out. Most people are looking for attention or a slice of the million dollar reward that Mr. Patterson posted—"

"My assistant was murdered!" Paul interrupted Mark.

"Oh my God! I'm so sorry," Mark replied earnestly.

Paul paused for a moment and replied: "Thank you. Her name was Alex. Alex Anderson."

"Wait," Mark interjected. "Wasn't Alex the person who encountered the man in the fedora in her dreams?"

"Yes, how did you know that?" Paul asked, eyebrows crunched.

"Pete…" Mark replied.

"Damnit!" Paul shouted. "He can't keep his big mouth shut. Fortunately, we were able to stop the dream monster. But, our bigger enemy — *SHE'S BACK.*"

"How do you know?" Mark asked with skepticism.

"I know she murdered Alex." Paul reached into his lab coat pocket and handed Mark a Japanese doll. "Look at the doll's tag." The following characters were printed on the tag: 花子さんの財産.

"It's in Japanese, but I recognize these characters: *Property of Hanako-San*," Mark said.

"Yes," Paul said. "I found this doll among all the packages in the living room."

"Isn't that crime scene evidence?" Mark inquired.

"Yes, but I didn't want it bagged up and lost. It may help us — along with this." Paul took out his phone and showed Mark a photo of the long mirror with the diagonal crack.

"That's the mirror from Jamie and Shelly's dorm room! How did you find it?" Mark asked anxiously.

"It's a long story, Mark. But, look closer." Paul zoomed in on the image to show Mark the words in blood red: "Bring Me Mary."

"Mary?" Mark asked.

"Yes, I think she's looking for Mary Montgomery," Paul replied.

"Little Mary? Well, I guess she's, what, 21 now?"

"Yes, she's an intern at my lab! She moved to California in 2018 and is a psychology prodigy. I need your help to understand why she's being targeted."

"Paul, there are a lot of people named 'Mary.' How do we know it's Mary Montgomery that she's after?"

"I don't. But that's why I need your help…"

Mark paused and then shook his head. "No, Paul. I can't. I'm picking up the pieces, moving on with my life…"

"No one has to know, Mark." Paul softened his tone. "I'm recruiting you for PattersonX! Allan has given me free rein to involve anyone I want in the mind-body problem project."

Mark sighed and then asked: "Well, what does this have to do with Jamie?"

"Take a look at this video. It was recorded at the house I own in Palo Alto. I have researchers live here as a company perk." Paul opened the video doorbell footage from his phone. He fast-forwarded to the scene where the woman appeared at the door.

"Oh my God, that is Jamie!" Mark gasped. "But, we saw this before; back when Shelly saw 'The Woman in White' in the dorm room…"

"Exactly," Paul agreed. "My suspicion is that Hanako-san 'appears' as Jamie on video. She's doing this to fool us."

"Well, what are the authorities saying?" Mark asked. "And, did anyone tell the Pattersons?"

"The authorities are baffled. They want to bring in the woman from the video for questioning. There is no direct evidence — no finger prints — nothing showing 'Jamie' did anything. Given how many 'Jamie sightings' there have been over the last seven years, the Detective does not want to say anything to the Pattersons until they know *for sure*. By the way, guess who is the lead on this case? Adam Scott, from the Mary Montgomery disappearance! You see how this is all adding up?"

Mark sighed.

"Look, Mark. I know you are trying to move on. I do respect that, believe it or not. I have a 4-bedroom apartment here in Columbus. I hid the mirror and the doll in my car before I called the police and quickly had them shipped here. So the police don't know anything about the mirror or the doll. I bought a plane ticket for Mary Montgomery to come out here as well. You don't have to travel. *No one has to know anything…*"

———

"Mark!" Shelly yelled as she saw Mark leave the phone room with Paul. "Have a moment?"

"I'll see you later, Mark." Paul nodded at Mark and left him to talk to his friend.

"Hey, what's up?" Mark asked with a small sigh.

"Oh, umm. Is everything okay?" Shelly didn't want to be nosy, but she was always the "queen of gossip" — ever since grade school.

"All good! Um, Paul wants me to join his 'mind-body problem' project. It's actually really awesome! Unfortunately, I am under a strict NDA. He wanted to go over that and have me sign it."

Shelly knew Mark well enough to tell when he was stretching the truth, but she didn't want to create any tension, especially since there was a hint that Mark may be interested in her beyond friendship.

"Okay. Well, I was wondering... a group of us are going out for some drinks after work. Wanna join us?" Shelly asked hopefully.

"Oh, I am so sorry; Paul wants to get started ASAP. Can I take a rain check?"

Mark saw the disappointment on Shelly's face. He reached over to her and gave her a hug.

"Hey, I'll see you on Monday. We'll have lunch, for sure. And, if I can squeeze in some time next weekend, would you like to see a movie?"

Shelly's mood changed immediately. "Yes! I would love that."

"Okay! Think about what you want to see. See you Monday." Mark walked away from Shelly and immediately turned his focus to everything Paul discussed. "Bloody Mary," Mark thought. "We are going to silence you — *for good!*"

CHAPTER 6

"Y ou are going *where*?" Ross Montgomery gave Mary a stern look as she began packing.

"Dr. Yang needs me to go to Columbus for a project with PattersonX. We may have a breakthrough with the 'mind-body problem.'" Mary stretched the truth a bit as she didn't want her dad worrying.

"But, Mary, *Alex Anderson was murdered*. She was murdered in the house *you* were going to stay at. I mean, what if you are in danger, too?" Ross sat down on Mary's bed as he watched her pack.

Mary paused for a moment. It was finally time to get the truth from Ross.

"Maybe I am in danger, Dad?" Mary stated boldly. "Maybe 'Bloody Mary' wants to capture me *again*…?"

Ross was taken aback by the statement. "What? What are you talking about, Mary?"

"You heard me, Dad. I was missing for two weeks. I wasn't taken by a 'cult' was I?" Mary's eyes began to water. "I need to know the *truth*." Mary sat next to Ross and held his hands.

"Okay, Mary. You are an adult now. Maybe it's time I tell you. Yes, on May 20, 2017, you went missing. We uncovered, with the help of the local Sheriff's office and two teens, that you had been abducted by Hanako-san, also known as 'Bloody Mary.' I can't believe I am actually saying this — she was an urban legend, but I guess some legends are grounded in the truth. There appears to be some portal. Apparently, the man you hold in such high regard, Dr. Scott Collier, may have opened this portal by mistake in March of 2017, two months before your disappearance. Scientists have theorized for centuries that there is some 'multiverse.' But now we know it's real — all of it."

Ross paused for a moment, as he had been rehearsing this in his mind for years, and it was such a relief to get it off his chest.

"When you were gone for the two weeks, you were in another dimension. Time, as you know it here on this Earth, did not exist there. From your perspective, you were gone for a split second.

"The Sheriff's department felt it necessary to keep this under wraps. If word got out, it would change the course of humanity. They didn't feel people were ready for this revelation, so it was best to stay silent and make up the story about the cult."

Mary hugged Ross. "Thank you, Dad, for being honest with me. I still don't remember anything that happened when I was in this other dimension. In a way, that may be a blessing in disguise. Who knows what Hanako-san had in store for me?" Mary shivered thinking about it.

"Don't worry, Dad. I promise to stay safe while I am away. I'll leave you my address and will have my phone with me at all times." Mary gave her dad one more hug.

"You have a good head on your shoulders, and *I trust you*." Ross let out a sigh. "But, please, Mary, come back home safely."

———

Ross dropped Mary off at San Francisco International Airport. It was crowded as always, but Paul upgraded Mary to First Class as a gesture of gratitude. As a result, she was able to make her way through security quickly. Mary parked herself at a table where she could use her laptop as she waited for her boarding group to be called.

As she waited at the gate, Mary couldn't help but notice a peculiar-looking man who seemed to be watching her. He was Caucasian, average height, and had thick gray hair. He wore a dark turtleneck shirt and gray slacks. He sat at one of the chairs facing Mary's table. The man looked down at his phone and periodically glanced over at Mary.

Mary wasn't sure what to think at this point. Was he just some creepy old guy? But, oddly enough, he seemed somewhat familiar…

"At least I'm in a public place," Mary reconciled to herself.

She put on her headphones and attempted to block him from her mind. About ten minutes had passed, and Mary garnered some courage to look over to where the man was sitting — but he was gone!

"First Class passengers, get ready to board." The announcer called out Mary's boarding group. She quickly gathered up her things and headed to the line. Periodically, Mary turned her head and looked around, but there was no sign of the stranger.

Mary sat in her assigned seat by the window, and the other passengers followed suit. She couldn't help but wonder if the mystery man would be on her flight. The seat next to Mary remained empty.

"Miss, I'm Leya. What would you like to drink?" A tall, thin woman of African descent, possibly in her 30s, serviced the First Class cabin. She held a pen and notepad as she questioned Mary.

"Just water, please," Mary said calmly. "Um, Leya, I hope you don't mind me asking, but is the seat next to me going to be occupied?"

Before Leya could answer the question, the cabin lavatory door opened, and the stranger walked out and headed over to the seat next to Mary!

"Do you want your usual, Mr. Williams?" Leya asked as she gave a warm smile to the stranger.

"Yes, and, please... just call me Pete." The man stashed his carry-on bag in the upper bin while addressing the stewardess.

Once Mary heard his voice, she was able to put it all together.

"Oh my God! You're Pete Williams from *Things That Go Bump in the Night!*" Mary squealed.

"Right... and you're Mary Montgomery," Pete said, as he settled into his seat.

"Wait, you know who I am?" Mary asked in a hesitant tone.

"Well, you may have noticed that I kept looking at you; I knew you were heading to Columbus, but I wasn't sure if you were the same 'Mary Montgomery from Edenvale.' You look a lot different." Pete gave Mary a reassuring smile.

"Oh, yeah, my 'awkward years.'" Mary rolled her eyes. "But, how did you get on this plane? I didn't even see you board. And, how did you know I would be on this flight?" Mary looked inquisitively at Pete.

"Geez, lots of questions. I like it!" Pete smiled. "I pre-boarded; part of the Million Mile Club. Been doing a lot of travel over the last seven years. Paul Yang invited me; he told me you would be on this flight."

"Oh, I see," Mary said in realization. "Well, what does Paul want from you?"

Pete hesitated but lent an answer. "It's time to stop *her*, once and for all. And, I think we finally know how to do it."

Leya arrived with Pete's drink and Mary's bottle of water.

"Here's your Bloody Mary, Pete," Leya said with a smile. Mary looked at Pete in amusement.

"And here's your water, Miss."

"Wait." Pete grabbed the water bottle and turned to Mary. "You're 21 now, right? This is a long flight. Leya, can we get a *real* drink for Miss Montgomery?" Pete winked at Mary. Leya obliged and handed Mary a blood-red concoction.

"Water..." Pete rolled his eyes jokingly. "To the devil with false modesty." Pete held his drink to Mary for a toast.

Mary laughed while toasting: "To the devil!"

Mary coughed as she sipped the strong beverage. "Um, can I just stick with water?" Mary asked as she continued to cough. Pete let out a laugh.

———

Over the course of the flight, Pete briefed Mary on the search for Jamie — seven years of dead-end leads. "I was ready to give up on the search," Pete explained, "but then I heard from Paul. Terrible what happened to Alex, but this is the break we've been looking for."

"Pete, did Paul tell you about Dr. Collier's video?" Mary asked.

"Woah, *what video*?" Pete asked in shock.

Mary grabbed her backpack and pulled out the thumb drive, headphones, and laptop. She inserted the thumb drive into the laptop and loaded the video. Mary handed her laptop and headphones to Pete.

Pete watched the video in dismay. "*Bring me Mary?*" Pete questioned as he took off the headphones.

"Yes!" Mary shouted. "But, that's not everything. Slow down the last 10 seconds, and tell me what you see."

Pete followed Mary's instructions and only saw static. "I don't see anything, Mary."

"*What?!*" Mary asked anxiously. She grabbed the laptop from Pete. "It should be right… here…?" Mary looked shocked as there was nothing but static…

CHAPTER 7

Paul invited Mark to his high-rise apartment in downtown Columbus. Although Mark agreed to assist, he resolved that this would be the *last time*. Mark's future looked bright — a great gig at Patterson AI; a chance to further develop his relationship with Shelly — as much as he loved Jamie, it was time to close this case *for good*.

Mark took the elevator up to the twelfth floor. Classical music played as multiple people made their way on and off. Mark finally reached the top floor. He walked over to apartment 1287 and rang the doorbell.

A familiar young woman opened the door. "Mark! It's been forever!" Mary Montgomery greeted Mark with a warm smile. "Come on in."

"Mary? Mary Montgomery? Wow!" As he entered the apartment, Mark was taken aback by how different Mary appeared from when he last saw her: she was radiant and confident.

"Yeah, I know: I get that reaction a lot from people who knew me during my 'awkward phase...'" Mary let out a sigh but stayed in good spirits.

"You look amazing," Mark said as he hugged Mary. "And

congratulations on your academic success. Ross must be so proud."

"Thanks, Mark! Yes, he certainly is." Mary paused for a moment. Mark was like a brother she never had. They stayed in touch periodically after Mary was rescued. "We can catch up more later; the team is anxious to get started. Let's head to the war room."

"*War room*? Okay…" Mark furrowed his eyebrows as he followed Mary to a large room which looked like something out of a crime scene investigation: a map with pins and strings that connected points A to B; photos of Jamie, Alex, Paul's house, and Jamie's dorm room pinned to cork boards; the Japanese doll sat on the coffee table; and the mirror with the diagonal crack rested against one of the walls. While sitting on a luxurious sofa, two men discussed something softly while enjoying glasses of wine. The gray haired gentleman noticed Mark and Mary enter the room.

"Look who's here; the man who blocks my messages," Pete Williams said sarcastically as he stood up from the couch while still holding his wine glass.

"Okay, Pete…" Mark said hesitantly.

"Hahaha!" Pete laughed as he placed his wine glass on the table. "Give me a hug, bro!"

Mark rolled his eyes and hugged Pete in hesitation.

"Glad to have you back, man!" Pete shouted.

"I'm not 'back,' Pete," Mark said firmly. "As I told Paul, this is it. *One last time*…" Mark looked over to the other man on the couch as he spoke the words.

Paul stood up from the couch.

"Glad you came over, Mark," Paul said as he shook Mark's hand.

"Please, have a seat." Paul motioned to Mark to have a seat on the sofa. "Would you like a glass of wine?" Paul offered to Mark. Mark politely declined.

"Mary has an important video to show us," Paul said as he

looked over at Mary. "I haven't seen it yet, but both Mary and Pete have."

Mary connected her laptop to the 70-inch wall mount television in the war room. "To give you some context, Mark," Mary interjected, "we are about to show you a video from Dr. Scott Collier: the night of his death."

"How were you able to get a hold of that?" Mark asked as he sat on one of the couches in the room.

"I found it in a box back at Paul's lab in Palo Alto," Mary said. "Brace yourself; it's disturbing."

Mary loaded the video, and Mark and Paul watched as Dr. Collier explained the portal, unleashing evil, and the connection to Bloody Mary.

When the end of the video loaded, Mark noticed something odd. "Wait! There was something in the last frame. Can you rewind, Mary?"

"Yeah! I thought I saw something, too, but it wasn't there when I showed this video to Pete on the airplane."

Mary slowed down the last few seconds, but this time it wasn't Bloody Mary...

"My God, that's Jamie!" Pete's jaw dropped. "Looks like she's saying something. Can we make it out?"

"I think she just said, 'Help!'" Paul said hesitantly.

Mary paused the video. "Wait! When I was at Paul's lab, I saw Bloody Mary in this final frame. She said, 'Bring me Mary.' And now, we are seeing Jamie Patterson asking for help?! *What does Bloody Mary want? What the hell is going on?* None of this makes sense!"

"Actually, it does. It makes perfect sense." A portly man with a gray beard entered the room. He wore a buttoned shirt and tan slacks. He slowly removed the hat from his head.

"Sheriff King?!" Mark shouted in amazement.

The Sheriff acknowledged Mark with a friendly nod.

"The 'Redneck Fox Mulder' is back! I thought you weren't

allowed to help us with Jamie's disappearance?" Pete asked curiously.

"Yes, and no. As of today, I am no longer 'Sheriff King.' You can now call me 'Detective King.' I retired from Waverly County and now work as a private investigator. An old friend, Detective Adam Scott, gave me a call and said you all were stuck. So, Paul here told me about this meeting place, gave me an entrance code, and here I am."

"Well, welcome to the investigation, *Detective* King," Mary said with a smile. "So why does all this make sense to you?"

"Kids, let's all sit down and get comfortable. It's time to go back to May 20, 1904 — the night *Mary Hunter* disappeared…"

CHAPTER 8

Edenvale, Ohio
May 20, 1904

"Y ou go up to the attic right now, young lady!" Mary Hunter was sound asleep when her mother yelled at her. Rosa Hunter Patterson had a difficult time sleeping, which was usually the case when her husband, Elias, was up late working. Rosa went into the kitchen and noticed her favorite tea cup was broken. She assumed it was Mary's fault, as Mary had been swinging her new doll around the kitchen that evening. The doll was a gift from Elias. He found the doll one day when he was cleaning the attic. It was exquisite — dressed in a kimono; it was most likely hand-crafted in Japan. He cleaned it up and gave it to Mary for her 13th birthday.

"I call her 'Little Mary,'" Elias mused as he handed the doll to his stepdaughter.

"I love it!" Mary said enthusiastically and hugged Elias. Rosa watched from the kitchen while the two were celebrating. Rosa was angered each time she saw Elias grow fonder of Mary — some sort of deep-rooted jealousy and fear.

"No! I don't want to go up there, Mother! It's scary!" Mary screamed back at Rosa.

Rosa grabbed Mary by the arm and dragged her out of bed. Mary held onto her doll as tight as she could while Rosa forced Mary down the hall and up the stairway. Rosa knew that Mary had a fear of the attic. In fact, Mary stated that she felt something or *someone* was watching her in the old garret, ever since she and her friends played "an old children's game" up there.

They reached the attic door. Mary tried hard to resist, but Rosa was able to lock Mary into the room.

"No, Mother, no!" Mary screamed in terror while facing the door. Mary was in tears and turned around slowly only to see the mirror right in front of her! Instead of Mary's reflection, she saw a *woman inside the mirror*! The woman had long, dark hair covering her face and wore a white gown. The woman's hand stretched out from inside the mirror to grab Mary! Mary screamed!

"Mary?" Rosa asked. "What's going on in there?" She was unable to open the door.

It was 3:33 AM, and Elias was in his outdoor workshop. He heard the commotion; in fact, even the neighbors heard the screams and joined Elias as they stormed into the house.

"Rosa?! Mary?!" Elias yelled.

"Help!" Rosa screamed out loud. Elias and his neighbors followed the sound to the upstairs attic. When they arrived, the attic door was open, and Rosa stood there in front of the mirror while holding "Little Mary" in her hands.

"Mary — Mary's gone! *She* took her!" Rosa explained as her face turned ghostly white…

CHAPTER 9

"So, 'Bring me Mary' really means 'Bring me the doll?'" Mary Montgomery asked.

"Exactly," Detective King said as he took the Japanese doll from the coffee table and made himself comfortable on the sofa. "Hanako-san wanted Mary's doll. There were a series of these dolls made; hand-crafted in Osaka, Japan. They were Hanako-san's playthings: Muffy, Buffy, Duffy, and this one. We don't have a name for it, other than *Little Mary*. It serves as a talisman. With it, Bloody Mary can jump to *any portal* in *any dimension* — *on any Earth* — *without being summoned.*

"Wait, you are talking about the multiverse," Mary said surprisingly. "So *it is* true."

"Welcome to the club, Mary," Paul said with a smile. "Scott and I hypothesized about this for years…"

"Yes, young Mary," Detective King interjected. "Ross called this morning and told me that he revealed the *real* reason why you went missing years ago. I don't know if you ever heard the term *ontological shock*? Well, we were afraid that most people would not be able to handle the truth; hence, the 'cult' cover story."

"It's been a lot to absorb," Mary asserted, "but I *needed* to know the truth — especially now."

"Understood, Miss Mary." Detective King let out a sigh.

"To continue with the doll... This specific doll became the talisman, as it was there with Hanako-san the day she was *murdered*. She was found dead in her school's restroom on the 3rd floor in stall number 3 on the 3rd day of the month..."

"Three thirty-three: the Witching Hour," Pete affirmed.

"Do we know what happened to the other dolls?" Mary asked.

"I know the answer," Pete said. "I have had reports on my show about mischievous Japanese dolls that have resulted in disappearances or possibly *murder*."

"Ugh, how creepy!" Mary shivered.

"Mary, don't go down that rabbit hole." Mark shoved his right elbow into Pete.

"Ow!" Pete pouted at Mark.

"Okay — I have a *real* question for you, Detective King," Mark said as he gave Pete an annoyed look. "Where has she been over the last seven years? Pete and I have been on so many wild goose chases, but we haven't seen Bloody Mary."

"I'm trying to figure that out as well," Detective King answered. "I suspect this mirror holds the clue." The detective pointed at the large mirror that was once in Jamie and Shelly's dorm room. "Where did you all find it?"

"Well, I can answer that one," Paul declared to the group. "We had a visiting scholar from Ohio State for a few months. She brought over a number of items that she was researching. Her interest was in the occult. I was a bit hesitant, but I let her bring over what she needed for her research. I had no idea that she was in possession of this specific mirror and the doll. She headed to Tahoe over winter break and died in a tragic ski accident. Her family only requested a few things to be returned. Alex was tasked with going through the remaining items and scheduling junk pickup or donation. I had no clue as to how she obtained the items. I asked her assistants and colleagues, but no one seemed to have any information.

"Detective King," Paul continued, "why did Alex have to die? What made Bloody Mary want her dead?"

"That is also a mystery. But, folks, we may be able to get our answer soon. Did you all get enough sleep? I have a feeling we'll have a friend appear in that mirror over yonder at 3:33 AM!"

"Jamie?" Mark asked.

"Yes, young Mark. When you all heard Miss Jamie say *'Help,'* she's actually saying she wants to help *us*…"

———

Mary, Paul, and Pete decided to take quick naps, while Detective King and Mark continued to talk.

"Why this specific mirror, Detective King? I thought the main portal was in Beth Reese's room — the one that was in the Patterson family for years and even took Mary Hunter?"

"Young Mark, do you know if Bloody Mary has been summoned prior on *this mirror*?"

"Oh no!" Mark realized. "Shelly's graduation party. Jamie was in the bathroom and a group of us played the Bloody Mary game. Oh, God, it's all our fault!"

"Don't blame yourself, young Mark. You didn't know. We'll get to the bottom of it."

———

It was 3:33 AM, and the group gathered around the mirror.

"What can we expect?" Paul asked Detective King after stretching and letting out a yawn.

"Soon we should have a glimpse into where Jamie has been captured. Let's hope she's there and in a safe space to talk with us."

As Detective King finished his sentence, the mirror changed

from being a reflection of the war room to a window into Jamie's dorm room. It appeared almost exactly how she and Shelly decorated it.

"Hello? Miss Jamie?" Detective King asked the mirror.

"Sheriff King?" A young woman's voice called out. "Is that you?"

"Yes, yes it is. I go by Detective King now. Is that you, Miss Jamie?"

Suddenly, in front of the mirror, Jamie Patterson appeared. Mark recognized her immediately; she was wearing the exact same outfit she wore on their final video call that fateful day in October 2017. She was as beautiful as ever.

"Jamie! I'm here, too!" Mark couldn't help but reach out.

"Mark! Mark!" Jamie yelled. "I can't see you. The mirror is foggy. I can hear you and Detective King! Who all is there with you?"

"Miss Jamie, we have myself, Mark, Mary Montgomery, Pete Williams from *Things That Go Bump in the Night*, and Dr. Paul Yang, a parapsychologist. We are all here to help."

"I don't have much time. I don't know when she's going to come back. I know you all probably have tons of questions, and I want to help!" Jamie shouted back to the team behind the foggy mirror.

"Yes, we do have some questions. First, Jamie, are you hurt or injured?" Detective King asked.

"I am not hurt. In fact, The Woman in White — I've been told to not use the *other* name — *needs me alive*. When traveling outside the mirror, she has to project as someone in human form. I agreed for her to use me if it meant protecting all of you."

"That's probably why she's been silent for over the last seven years," Pete declared.

"Seven years?" Jamie asked. "I feel as if I have only been here a few hours."

"Yes, Jamie," Pete interjected. "Time, as we know it here on Earth, is a construct that may not exist in your new reality."

"Jamie, you said that we would be protected. Well, then why was Alex Anderson murdered?" Paul's voice trembled as he asked the question.

"The Woman in White made a deal with some shadowy figure. A man who wears a fedora..."

"Oh my God!" Pete said as he and Paul looked at each other. "The man who haunts people in their sleep..."

"He wanted her to obtain Alex's dreamcatcher so he could take her soul in her sleep. In exchange, he promised to lead her to a Japanese doll. It's a special doll she had as a child. He told her it was located in the house in which Alex was staying. The Woman in White can only stay in human form for a short period of time. She searched frantically but was not able to locate it. Enraged, she didn't complete her deal with the man in the fedora. Instead, she sought revenge: *The Woman in White murdered Alex*." Jamie let out a big sigh.

"I am so sorry for your loss. She seemed like a wonderful person," Jamie said with deep sympathy.

"Thank you, Jamie," Paul replied.

"Well, Miss Jamie, we acquired the doll. However, The Woman in White stayed long enough to use your image on camera. The police are suspecting *you* in the murder of Alex Anderson."

"I guess it serves me right for making a deal with the devil," Jamie said quietly.

"No, don't blame yourself," Mark consoled Jamie. "Look, this may actually all be *my fault*..." Mark confessed.

"No, young Mark," Detective King attempted to stop him.

"No, she needs to hear this," Mark demanded.

"Hear what, Mark?" Jamie asked with concern.

"The night of the graduation party — at Shelly's — when you went to the bathroom, a group of us played the game. We summoned The Woman in White through this very mirror. This is all my fault."

"No, Mark," Jamie replied with deep concern. "It's not your

fault. You couldn't have known. *This woman is evil.* She finds a way to get what she wants."

"Jamie, it's Mary Montgomery. I am forever grateful for you, Mark, and Detective King for all your help in my safe return. I owe you so much, Jamie. What can I do to help?"

"That's very sweet, Mary," Jamie replied. "But I think there is only one way to end this. Please, hand me the doll so I can destroy it. And then close this portal for good."

"There has to be another way, Jamie," Pete argued.

"Actually, Miss Jamie is right," Detective King countered. "Destroying the talisman in Hanako-san's home dimension should break the curse and will render her powerless. Jamie can still survive in this alternative reality. Bringing her back to *our reality* will just cause—"

"*Ontological shock*," Mary replied.

"Exactly." Detective King nodded.

Mark moved close to the mirror. "Jamie, you know I will always love you. I understand what you have to do. There was not a single day that went by when I didn't think about you. But knowing that you will be safe, even though we will be apart, will make me happy."

"Mark, my love, I want you to be happy, too. You have a great support system there. It's my time to do something greater than myself. Be sure to tell my parents that I love them."

Jamie reached her hand through the mirror. Tearfully, Detective King handed the doll to Jamie.

"When I shout out to you, crush this mirror immediately!" Jamie demanded. "She's going to come back here soon; she will be able to sense that I have the doll. Get ready."

Paul had several sledgehammers ready, as he suspected that at some point the mirror would need to be destroyed. He, Pete, and Mark stood on guard as they waited for Jamie's signal.

———

Jamie waited patiently in her room, as she listened for Bloody Mary. She opened the dorm room door and the hallway lights began to flicker. A shadowy figure proceeded down the hallway. It began moaning. It was The Woman in White.

"Bring. Me. Mary." Bloody Mary began to chant while also growling. "Bring. Me. Mary!"

Jamie shivered but stood her ground. "Come and get her!"

Jamie ran back into her room and stood on top of her desk. As Bloody Mary entered, Jamie had one hand on the doll's head and the other ready to rip it off its body.

"Not my Mary!" The Woman in White shrieked.

"Yes, it's time to die, bitch!"

Jamie ripped the doll apart and yelled to the mirror. "Destroy it now!"

Paul, Pete, and Mark heard Jamie's signal and immediately smashed the mirror.

Bloody Mary moaned in pain and tried to reach over to Jamie, but she crumbled to the ground. Her body began to wither, and then there was nothing left but the white gown.

"Finally, it's over," Jamie sighed.

CHAPTER 10

Oakridge Memorial Park
San Jose, California

A lex Anderson was more than a friend. She was the most giving person I had ever met…" Steph tried hard to hold back her tears as she gave the eulogy. It took place not too far from where Alex's parents were interred. In fact, not too far from the crypt of Dr. Scott Collier…

"This isn't the most enjoyable place for a first date, but I am glad you were able to make it out here to California." Mark held Shelly's hand as they sat and listened to Steph's memorial to Alex.

"It's okay, Mark. And thank you for telling me everything that happened. I think we are starting off on the right foot." Shelly smiled and rested her head on Mark's right shoulder.

Paul, Pete, Mary and Ross Montgomery, Alex's boyfriend Mike, Steph's boyfriend Ryan, and Alex's sister were all in attendance. There were a number of others who attended: former colleagues, Ed from the thrift store that Alex frequented, and a young, beautiful woman wearing a large hat.

Once the service concluded, a few of the guests gathered

around the garden near the mausoleum to catch up and have some drinks and light snacks.

"Hey, Paul, did you take Alex's dreamcatcher?" Pete whispered into Paul's ear and then sipped a glass of wine.

"I picked it up from Detective Scott before the memorial service." Paul patted his blazer pocket to indicate that the dreamcatcher was safe and sound.

Although it was a beautiful day in San Jose, it was quite windy. The napkins on the snack table began to fly away.

"I'll grab them!" Paul yelled as he attempted to rescue the napkins. As he turned, he accidentally bumped into the woman in the large hat. She had the most piercing green eyes. It caught Paul off-guard.

"Excuse me, Miss," Paul said politely.

"It's okay. A bit crowded. I was just leaving."

"Well, thanks for coming." Paul watched as the stunning woman left for her ride share, a red Tesla Model X.

"Wowza! Who was *that*?" Pete asked Paul as they watched the Tesla leave the memorial park.

"I have no idea. I think Mary was in charge of the guest list."

Paul walked over to Mary and asked, "Hey, who was that woman in the large hat?"

"Oh, let me check." Mary unlocked her tablet to browse the list. "I think her name was 'Genevieve.'"

"What?!" Paul yelled.

"Oh shit. Check your jacket pocket!" Pete urged.

"It's gone. The dreamcatcher is gone..."

Patterson AI Headquarters
Columbus, Ohio

It seemed like just another day at Patterson AI. Allan Patterson was in the office to get the latest revenue forecast from the

Finance team. While he waited, he received a page from his assistant.

"Mr. Patterson, you have a visitor: Detective King."

"Detective King?" Mr. Patterson was puzzled.

"Yes, he said you may know him as *Sheriff* Andy King of Waverly County. He investigated *Miss Jamie*'s accident seven years ago?"

"Ah, yes, please send him to my office."

Mr. Patterson stood up from his desk as he watched his assistant guide Detective King. He opened his office door and greeted the Detective.

"*Detective* King; did they demote you?!" Mr. Patterson said with a laugh.

"Nope, no demotion here. I retired from the Sheriff's Department and now work as a private investigator." Detective King answered as he walked into the office.

"Nice! So, to what do I owe this pleasure? Please have a seat. Would you like some coffee?"

"Oh no thank you, Mr. Patterson. This will be a short visit."

"Okay then, but call me Allan," Allan said with a smile. "Janet, please close the door on your way out."

Allan's assistant closed the door behind the detective.

"I don't know how to say this, but I will be direct. Miss Jamie is alive," Detective King said earnestly.

"What now? She is?! Where? Where is she? Have you seen her?" Allan shot out of his chair in an anxious joy.

"Mr. Allan. There is a lot more. Please, sit."

"Okay. If she's alive, that's great news, *isn't it*?" Allan questioned the detective.

Instead of answering the question, Detective King posed his own question. "Have you heard the term *ontological shock*?"

EPILOGUE

From the Journal of Jamie Patterson

I am trapped in this place that looks like Earth but doesn't feel the same. I am now Jamie Patterson of this new dimension. I am starting to remember things about this specific existence. My parents are Allan and Jenny Patterson, but Jenny died when I was born. I have a step-mother; her name is Janet. Allan doesn't have a robotics company; instead, he's a school teacher. Janet is a writer.

Shelly is still my roommate, but she only knows THIS version of "Jamie." Apparently, Shelly is very shy and would prefer to stay indoors. Quite the contrast from the OTHER Shelly who couldn't wait to pledge with the Tri-Delts... Her boyfriend is Steve. Yeah, Steve the "plus one."

The memories of my old life have been fading fast. I think I may have had a boyfriend. I remember that he was really smart, and I think he went to school in California. I can't really ask Shelly; she'll think it's weird that I don't remember my current life. The yearbooks are helping a bit. I guess I don't have a boyfriend? Oh well. I'll take this journal with me as I head over to Starbucks (they still exist here; thank God!).

I walked over to the campus Starbucks. The young man who took my order was very nice. His name tag said his name was "Mark." He was tall and had sky blue eyes…

ABOUT THE AUTHOR

Growing up loving horror and mystery tales, JC Bratton writes stories that pay homage to the Point Horror novels she would read as a kid: stories such as *Slumber Party* by Christopher Pike and *Twisted* by RL Stine. Some of her biggest influences are Alfred Hitchcock, Lois Duncan, Stephen King, and Richard Matheson.

Although she hopes for that Netflix movie deal, JC still has her day job and lives in the heart of Silicon Valley with her husband, stepsons, and cats.

amazon.com/author/jcbratton
youtube.com/@jcbratton

ALSO FROM BLUE MILK PUBLISHING

Blue Milk Publishing represents independent authors of both fiction and non-fiction works.

*Please visit **bluemilk.co** for more information.*

Non-Fiction

The Cheating Boyfriend (And Other Organizational Indiscretions) (January 2017) by Jenny Hayes Carhart, MSOD, PHR

Fiction

Who's at the Door? (January 2020) by JC Bratton

Parasomnia (June 2020) by JC Bratton

Dollhouse (October 2020) by JC Bratton

Who's Back at the Door? (October 2023) by JC Bratton

JC Bratton's Things That Go Bump in the Night, Volume One: Urban Legends (October 2023) by JC Bratton